TRAIN TO THE PAST

TASNIM SULTHANA

Made with ♥ on the Notion Press Platform
www.notionpress.com

I dedicate this book to my hard work and my unwavering 'never give up' attitude, which have always helped me climb the mountains of success, even in the darkest of times.

Contents

Contents

Acknowledgements

I would like to thank my best friend, Shalini Shinde, and my sister, Tahsin Sulthana, for their constant support, encouragement, and invaluable feedback whenever I needed it.

CHAPTER ONE

AN ODD JOB

A warm afternoon sun bathed the field as Steve tended to his horses. The crunch of footsteps on the grass startled him, and he spun around to find a man approaching. Steve squinted as the man approached. Short, stout, with dishevelled hair and clothes that looked like they hadn't seen a wash in days. The closer he came, the more Steve noticed—a slight limp, dark bags under his eyes, and the scent of cheap cologne mixed with something... rotten.

"John," the man said, his voice gruff and low, like gravel grinding beneath a heavy boot. The man was in his fifties. What he said next dazed Steve.

"There's a girl we need you to find," John said flatly, his words delivered without emotion. "The reward is substantial."

Steve, barely thirty, blinked in confusion.

"What?" he muttered.

John repeated his offer and waited.

"Find a girl?" Steve scoffed, trying to mask his unease. "That's not my line of work." He turned back to his horses.

"I'd think twice before turning down this offer," John said, his eyes narrowing. "It's not every day someone in your situation gets a chance like this."

Steve frowned. "My situation?"

John tilted his head. "Small town, low wages, a brother with college dreams. You think people don't notice?"

Steve's pulse quickened but he chose to act cool in front of the stranger.

So, he just said, "I think you came looking for the wrong person. Anyway, nice talking to you. Now, if you'll excuse me, I have work to do."

His voice wavered despite his attempt to sound tough.

"Arrogant lad." John muttered, his eyes narrowing like he could glimpse right through his facade. "I'm just a messenger and this is what I've been told to inform you: if you want to accept the deal, come to this place tomorrow at 2 p.m. sharp."

John's hand slipped into his jacket, pulling out a small, crumpled piece of paper.

Steve stared at it—such a small thing, yet it seemed to carry the weight of something far bigger.

When John handed it over, Steve hesitated. The paper felt worn and damp between his fingers, the ink smeared from rough handling. His thumb traced the address, each stroke setting off a fresh wave of unease.

"If you're smart and know what's good for you, you'll accept the deal." John added, his voice cutting through the thickening silence. Steve's gaze flicked up, catching the glint of something on John's wrist—a strange, dark mark peeking out from under the cuff of his sleeve. John tugged it back quickly, clearing his throat, but Steve couldn't shake the feeling he'd seen something he wasn't supposed to.

"Come to this place tomorrow, 2 p.m. Don't be late." And he left.

Steve kept looking at him as the man walked away. After a while, he got back to his work. Steve was tall and handsome with sharp jawline. Though he had a lean body, his blonde hair and blue eyes always attracted lot of girls. Steve had a younger brother named Charlie. He was five years younger to him.

While Steve sat next to his horse to rest, he felt as if it was yesterday his parents were going to work and left Charlie with him. He used to take care of him and feed him. He was more of a parent to him than a sibling. So, he felt a deep sense of guilt as he was not able to send his brother to college for further studies. After their parents died, Steve had started working at a library.

Steve and Charlie lived in Whispering Pines in the countryside of eastern Canada, outside of Silverleaf city.

They lived in a small one room building made of rocks. The horses he had were given to him by a rich man in return of a favor he had done for him. Whispering Pines had a stillness about it, a quiet that made the town feel suspended in time.

The rolling hills on the outskirts were thick with towering pines and maple trees. The scent of pine needles mixed with the faint smell of woodsmoke as chimney stacks puffed lazily into the cool afternoon air.

The town's few streets were lined with aging wooden buildings, their facades worn from years of harsh winters and bright summers. Whispering Pines might be small, but its simplicity held both a charm and a sense of isolation—perfect for hiding secrets.

That night, Steve was in bed watching his brother sleep. He glanced at the dusty textbooks piled in the corner, remnants of dreams set aside for bills and groceries. The offer gnawed at Steve all night, an itch he couldn't scratch. He'd lie in bed, eyes squeezed shut, but sleep refused to come.

He stared at the ceiling, mind racing, replaying every word John had said. Steve rolled over, pressing his face into the pillow. He could say no.

Forget this whole thing, pretend it never happened. He didn't owe these people anything but the thought of Charlie—stuck in this dead-end town while his friends were off starting their lives—ate at him, clawing at his resolve.

By morning, Steve's decision felt as heavy as the sunrise creeping through the window.

He needed to try. How could he ask Charlie to keep waiting, keep hoping?

The weight of it all pressed on Steve's chest—he had to do something. This might be his only shot at changing their lives, no matter how dangerous it seemed.

It was 1PM and it was a 45 mins ride from his house to the address that was given.

He gave it a final thought and decided to go.

The paper mill loomed in front of him, its weathered walls sagging under the weight of time. The smell of damp wood and rust clung to the air.

Steve stepped through the creaking gate, his boots crunching on brittle, dead leaves. A gust of wind whistled through the broken windows, sending a chill down his spine. His heart skipped when he saw five masked figures standing by a car, their imposing frames casting long shadows. Fear gripped him.

He wanted to turn back and run for his life. Before he could do it, a voice spoke from the five. "Steve, we're glad that you decided to come."

The sound was muffled due to the mask but even then, Steve could sense that it was a deep, firm and commanding voice that could only belong to a leader.

Steve didn't respond. Steve's legs felt like lead, each breath shallow and quick.

His heart thundered in his chest, a wild drumbeat that drowned out the wind's whistle.

He couldn't tear his eyes away from the masked men, their cold, silent stares burning into him. What were they waiting for?

He glanced around, half-expecting someone to jump out of the shadows. But nothing. Only the low hum of the wind pushing through the cracked windows. One of the figures shifted, and Steve couldn't tell if it was a threat or just impatience. Either way, it sent a jolt through his spine. The man continued in his commanding voice.

"We have a simple task for you. We need you for something. There's a girl, and if you find her, you'll be rewarded."

Steve finally found his voice. He said, "Why did you choose me and how come you know so much about me? What makes you think I can find her? Why not go to the police? This sounds... risky."

"We'll let you know all that you are required to know to complete the task but first we need to know if you are ready to accept the deal."

Steve's mind raced. The reward dangled before him like an escape from his problems—Charlie's future, his own debts—but what was the cost?

He glanced at the masked figures, their silence unnerving. Was this the kind of job that could get him killed?

"What happens if I fail?" Steve asked, his voice tight with anxiety. The leader's reply was swift and emotionless.

"That's not an option."

Steve swallowed hard. He could feel it in his gut, that creeping sense that this was more than just a "simple task." No, it was more like a trap. Should he just involve police? As this thought popped in his head, Charlie's face flashed in his mind.

"We don't have all day, you know. We'll give you 5 minutes to think." Said the one on the extreme right.

Steve looked at the men, his throat tight. This was insane. He didn't know these people, didn't know the job, or if they could be trusted.

His mind whirled with questions, fear clawing at his chest. Could he really risk their safety for a chance at a better life? He was about to say no to them but the weight of responsibility pressed down, suffocating him.

His stomach twisted. There was a long silence before he answered. In that silence he remembered his mom's last words where she asked him to take care of his brother and he imagined his brother in white coat attending to patients.

After what felt like an eternity, he whispered, "Okay."

The word felt like a death sentence. They all looked at each other and nodded in satisfaction.

The man in the middle spoke again. "We'll give you a map. If you follow it, you'll reach the place marked in red on the map. You'll know what to do once you reach there."

He handed him the map.

Steve asked, "I'll need a photo of the girl I'll be looking for."

The man in the middle laughed and said, "There's no photo of her."

Steve was annoyed to hear this. He said, "How am I supposed to find the girl if I don't know how she looks?"

To which the man replied, "You'll know when you see her."

CHAPTER TWO

THE TRAIN

The sun blazed high, yet an unsettling chill lingered as Steve headed toward the red mark on the map, his mind still tangled in the cryptic conversation with the masked men. He didn't really get to have a conversation with Charlie about the whole incident because he was out with his friends for the weekend. So, Steve just left a note for him saying he would return soon from an urgent errand that had unexpectedly come up.

The place mentioned on the map was 40 km west to the town. The place was marked with lot of trees. So, Steve assumed it would be a forest there. It was almost noon when he reached the place. To his complete bewilderment, the land stretched out before him, utterly void of life, save for a single, solitary tree standing eerily in the centre—an odd and haunting presence in the endless, forsaken expanse.

The silence that filled the space was unnerving; even the wind seemed to be still in this place.

It gave an eerie feeling that Steve couldn't brush off. He had no idea how being in an open field would help him find that girl. Exhausted from the journey, Steve decided to rest under the tree for a while.

He had barely touched the bark of the tree when it felt strangely warm beneath his fingertips, and before he could process it, the landscape began to shift.

One by one, trees flickered into existence as though conjured from a distant memory. Soon, he found himself standing in the middle of a dense forest except that the trees weren't green.

They had golden leaves and silver branches. Steve stood frozen, a surge of adrenaline hit him, as the once barren land transformed into an enchanted forest, silent and watchful. He stood there for a moment in complete awe at the mind-boggling transformation that had taken place before his eyes. As he reached out, the trees seemed to recoil, their branches bending unnaturally, retreating like shadows in the light and that's when he realized the trees were creating a path for him to follow.

Not knowing what lay ahead, he took a deep breath and started following the path reluctantly. All along the path, the trees looked like strong pillars burying a treasure below them. The scene looked something from a fairyland. He kept moving forward. Each step he took made him anxious. His mouth went dry whenever he imagined what he would find at the end of the path. He eventually realized that his watch stopped working as soon as the forest had emerged. So, he could only assume that he was walking for almost an hour and still couldn't see the end. He continued his journey. After what seemed like an eternity, he saw a clearing ahead of him. It was an open space with what looked like a really old rusty train standing in the middle on wooden tracks that started abruptly in the middle.

He moved forward to examine the train more closely. He almost fainted after seeing what was written on the train. He stumbled back, breath caught in his throat, as his eyes locked on the words scrawled in dark, dripping letters: TRAIN TO THE PAST.

They shimmered in the mist like a bad dream. Steve blinked, half-convinced it would disappear—but it didn't. That's when he noticed the train itself, as if seeing it for the first time.

The train stood silent at the edge of the forgotten station, cloaked in a thick mist that seemed to hang heavier around its rusted frame. As he started examining the train, he found himself intrigued and fascinated along with a deep sense of awe. The train's once gleaming steel had turned a deep, reddish-brown, a patchwork of decay etched into every surface. Massive iron wheels, jagged with age, rested on cracked tracks that hadn't seen life in decades.

Suspicion and Paranoia kicked in when he noticed the structure of the train. Unlike any regular train, its body was twisted—almost serpentine—its carriages tapering into strange, crooked angles, as though time itself had warped its shape.

He was overwhelmed with fear when he heard the faint whispers that seemed to echo from within, carried on the wind like voices from another time.

The windows, clouded with grime, flickered with brief glimpses of scenes from the past—old towns, forgotten faces, distant memories. Ironically, the voices and the memories flickering made him realise the isolation that was wrapping up this place. He was suddenly aware of his breath and his heartbeat.

Steve's eyes darted around the station. Nothing. The once-clear path he had followed was swallowed by the fog, leaving him stranded. His heart pounded in his ears. *This can't be happening.* He spun in place, hoping for any sign of life—another way out. But there was nothing, just the mist, the train, and that cursed message. His breath hitched. He was trapped. There was no escape. Except... the train.

With no other way out, he gave in to the pull of the unknown and stepped forward, though his legs felt as heavy as stone. His breath quickened, his whole-body trembling—not from the cold but from the fear of what lay ahead.

Glancing back at the deserted station, he scanned the thick mist one last time.

No shadowy figure emerged to stop him; no voice called him back. He was alone. Reluctantly, he boarded the train. The door creaked shut behind him, sealing him inside. He hadn't even found his footing before the train lurched forward. His stomach dropped. There was no one driving it, of that, he was sure. His heart hammered in his chest as he realized the truth: the train was moving on its own. The controls—if they even existed—were hidden, but the eerie sense of being carried by something far beyond his understanding gnawed at him. Whatever force had set this in motion was now in control.

After the initial shock wore off, he finally looked around this strange train. The train's interior mirrored its serpentine shape, with narrow, winding corridors that twisted unnervingly, making it impossible to see what lay ahead.

A creeping sense of unease settled in his chest.

He thought he heard voices but when he looked around there was no one or at least, that's what he thought.

Steve felt a twinge of intimidation as the train swayed violently, throwing him against the walls that were dark and glisten like wet scales, reflecting dim, flickering lights that cast unsettling shadows. The seats were covered in an ancient, faded fabric, frayed at the edges, as though untouched for centuries. The air hummed with a spooky, low vibration. He looked outside the window and instead of showing landscapes it revealed swirling mists that seem to move backward in time. Every creak of the train felt alive, as if the very structure was shifting beneath him, whispering forgotten secrets of the past.

His legs trembled. As he reached for a seat, a sharp chill pierced through him, making his skin crawl.

He stumbled back, eyes widening at the pearly figure seated where he'd tried to rest.

It was human-shaped, yet ethereal, like a wisp of cloud. Glancing around, Steve realized every seat was occupied by these ghostly figures, gazing blankly into the void.

One seat remained empty. Was it for him? Exhausted, his body seemed to move on its own. He collapsed into the seat, and before he could question it, sleep overtook him.

CHAPTER THREE

INTO THE UNKNOWN

Steve woke up, his head heavy, as if he had been submerged in thick fog. His limbs felt stiff, and a faint ringing echoed in his ears. He didn't know how long he was asleep or where he was. He suddenly realized that the train had stopped. The sudden, unnatural stillness of the train jolted him out of his daze. The faint hum of movement was gone, replaced by a creepy, suffocating quiet. He looked around and found that the pearly figures had vanished, leaving behind only the chill of their presence. Steve got up from his seat and started walking down the aisle. When he reached the door, he saw that it was open. Without thinking twice, he raced out of the door.

He stepped into total darkness. The air was damp and heavy, clinging to his skin like a wet shroud. Panic rose in his chest as he waved his hand in front of his face—nothing.

His breath quickened; the air thick with unease. He looked around frantically but couldn't see a thing.

He stood there in silence with sweat trickling down his neck, waiting for his eyes to adjust to the dark. Steve strained to hear something—anything—but the silence was oppressive, broken only by the faint shuffle of his own feet and the steady pounding of his heartbeat in his ears.

The ground beneath him felt uneven, gritty, as if he stood on loose dirt or gravel. Gradually, his eyes caught the silhouette of human body at a distance.

He hesitated for a moment but then started walking towards them.

As he drew closer, the murky forms solidified into men—silent, motionless—each tending to a table overflowing with strange jars.

The glass containers gleamed dully, but what lay inside was twisted beneath the dim light.

He asked one of the men, "What is this place?"

The man looked up at him and said in a low, mysterious voice, "Steve, you shouldn't have come here."

Steve was taken aback. Dread curled in his stomach.

The hairs on the back of his neck stood up, his body instinctively tense. He wasn't supposed to be here—he could feel it now.

He asked the man, "How do you know my name?"

The mysterious man scoffed, a sneer curling at the edge of his lips, his voice laced with condescension.

"How do I know?" he exclaimed in a proud voice. "This is the land of memories, you ignorant lad. We know every forgotten thing about everyone who ever existed on the planet of earth. It is we who have protected these memories since eternity."

Steve didn't know how to respond. His thoughts were whirling around in his head trying to make sense of everything that has been happening from the moment he had touched that tree. Steve formed his next words gingerly, trying to avoid any trouble with the man.

"So, if you know everything, you would also know about the girl I need to find. Is it possible for you to help me search for her?"

"Well, of course I know about the girl but I'm not at liberty to disclose any information. You know, we are bound by some rules that we need to abide by."

Steve felt disheartened at hearing this. He felt like he just went back to square one.

He said in a desperate voice, "If I was brought here by some power, it wants me to look for her here. There has to be something I could do to find her."

"I said I can't reveal any information. I never said I can't help you." the man said simply.

Steve didn't know what to make of those words. He just looked at him blankly for a moment.

Looking at the expression on Steve, the man chuckled and said, "These jars that you see here are filled with memories of the past. Each jar consists of a single memory. Some memories will help you reach your destination and others will mislead you."

Steve couldn't digest what he was hearing. Memories helping him find the girl? Is that possible? More importantly, is it plausible? It was absurd. And yet, after everything he had seen, how could he dismiss it? His grip tightened. What if this was his only chance?

The man continued, "You need to pay a price for each jar."

"I have enough money to buy a dozen memories, I suppose."

The man replied, "Money is not the price, Steve.

Steve's stomach twisted as the man's words sunk in. Not money? Then what?

The man's gaze lingered on him, cold and calculating. "Your memories, Steve," he said, each word heavy with consequence. "For every one you take, you give one back."

Steve couldn't take it anymore. This was insane. Memory in exchange of a memory? For a second there, he thought he was just having a bad dream that would disappear the moment he opened his eyes.

He pinched himself to wake up from this nightmare but to his dismay, nothing changed. He was still there standing in darkness in front of this strange man. Steve's mind raced.

What if he lost something he couldn't afford to forget? His mother's face, his first victory, the laughter of his friends—could he risk it?

What if he lost something he couldn't get back—something he didn't even realize he cherished?

He glanced at the jars lining the shelves, each one containing a fragment of someone's life.

Would his memories be trapped in one of those?

"You're joking," Steve stammered, his voice trembling as he searched the man's face for any sign of jest.

But the man's cold eyes remained fixed on him, unblinking, unsympathetic. "I don't joke," the man said, a thin smile creeping across his lips. "The price must be paid."

Steve had it enough. His mind, once sharp and determined, now throbbed with a dull ache as fear gnawed at the edges of his resolve. What was the point of finding her if it cost him his sanity? What if he didn't recognize himself by the end of this madness?

He spun around, sprinting toward the train, his only tether to the world he still knew. When he reached the spot, the train that had stood mere moments ago, disappeared, the tracks had vanished too—swallowed by the earth, leaving no trace.

The silence pressed down, thick and unnatural. He glanced around frantically, searching for any trace of the train.

It couldn't have vanished into nothingness—surely, it had to be here, hidden in the folds of this strange land. Yet, no matter where he looked, there was nothing. No tracks, no station, no sign of escape. Only the unsettling realization that crept in: he was trapped, with no way out.

The wind, which had been nothing more than a gentle breeze earlier, now howled through the air with an eerie whistle, carrying with it a distant hum, like the low drone of voices just out of reach.

The ground beneath Steve's feet felt unsteady, like walking on sand that threatened to swallow him whole. The sky, once a dull grey, seemed to ripple, as though the very fabric of reality was unravelling in front of his eyes.

His senses screamed that this was no place for the living. Something ancient lingered here, watching, waiting.

"Looking for the train?" The man's voice slithered from behind, calm, almost amused. "You can run all you like, but there's no going back. Not now. Not ever."

Steve's mouth went dry. "What do you mean?"

The man's grin widened, his eyes gleamed with an ancient knowledge, chilling certainty.

"Do you think you're the first to try? The last one who wandered here—what was it? A thousand years ago? You'll find him, still wandering. Just like you will. This place... it's no playground. It's sacred, and you've trespassed. Now, you'll get exactly what you deserve."

As Steve stood there, his legs trembling, he felt an unsettling shift, like the ground itself was moving beneath him, yet he hadn't moved at all. His watch ticked away, but when he glanced down, the hands spun wildly, out of control. He tried to count the seconds in his head, but time felt slippery, escaping his grasp. The sky flickered as if someone had flipped a switch. The strange land felt timeless, ageless—like he had been here forever, or maybe only a minute. He couldn't tell anymore.

CHAPTER FOUR

MEMORIES

"Come looking for me when you're ready."

Before Steve could say anything, the man started walking away and disappeared into the fog. Steve didn't know what to do next. Certainly, he couldn't just stand there for eternity. So, he started walking. He could make out the lining of buildings on one side. He started walking towards the one nearest to him. He wanted to rest for a while and if possible, find anything to eat.

He suddenly realized how hungry he was. His stomach growled, but the thought of food felt secondary to the creeping sense of wrongness curling in his chest. He reached the door of the first building. His eyes flicked over the building, something gnawing at him—something was wrong, but it took a few long seconds before it struck him. The building hovered, just inches off the ground. It looked eerie, like someone was hanging it from above. When he thought about everything that he had seen up until now, this didn't look as scary as he expected it to.

The cold bit into his skin, an icy breath brushing his neck, and the silence... it was more than quiet—it felt heavy, like something waiting to pounce. Steve blinked at the suspended building for a few moments and decided to go inside anyway. He knocked several times. He waited, every second stretching out, but no one came. Finally, with a hand he couldn't quite steady, Steve pushed against the door. It groaned as it opened, the sound cutting through the silence and sending a shiver through him.

He went inside. He saw in front of himself a long corridor with doors on either side.

The corridor itself was barely lit by a lantern on the wall giving the whole place a spooky look. There was a chandelier hanging from the ceiling in the middle of the corridor.

To his horror, he realized that it was made of human skulls. He let out a wild scream.

With heart still pounding fast in his chest, he looked at all the doors around him and decided to open the first door on his right.

The moment he opened the door, light exploded through the hallway, so bright that it was almost painful.

Steve shielded his eyes, heart pounding as the darkness dissolved into this new, impossible world. He entered the room. There was a positive vibe to it. The sun was rising from one end of the room. There were mountains that seemed far way. A small cottage in the open space. He took a step forward and something hit his head. He looked up to see several objects floating in the air. Toys and books drifted lazily above him, as if carried by an invisible breeze. A milk bottle spun slowly, suspended in midair. Everything in this space felt soft, unreal. He knew this was a happy place. He suddenly saw a women coming out of the cottage with a baby in her arms. When he saw the women's face, he was dumfounded. His breath caught in his throat. No, it couldn't be... But there she was, his mother, stepping out of the cottage, her smile soft and familiar. And in her arms—him. Baby Steve, cradled gently.

His mind spun; he rubbed his eyes, blinked hard, but the image didn't vanish. He couldn't believe his eyes. He reached out, fingers trembling, but they passed right through.

Only air. His heart sank—he was a ghost in this place, a mere observer. His mom was busy feeding baby Steve. It was as if she never died.

He couldn't stop staring, joy filling every inch of him, but beneath it, a deep ache formed. She looked so alive, so real, but he knew... knew she wasn't.

Leaving was the last thing on Steve's mind. He sank to the ground, knees weak beneath him. He didn't want to blink, afraid that if he did, she'd vanish. His mother—alive, vibrant—moved with a grace he'd forgotten, her soft smile the one he'd dreamed of seeing again for years. He watched as she cradled baby Steve, cooing softly, completely unaware of his presence. Every fibre of his being ached to call out to her again, to feel her touch, to hear her voice directed at him. But he couldn't. All he could do was sit and watch, eyes filling with tears. How many years had passed since he'd felt this kind of warmth? Since he'd felt truly loved.

He sat there for hours, watching his mom, adoring her.

Charlie was too young when their parents died. So, he didn't remember them well. Steve wished Charlie was here with him to see their mom. After watching her mother for some more time, heart heavy, he turned toward the door. A shadow shifted in the corner of the room. Steve's heart pounded as the figure stepped forward, and suddenly, he was staring into his own eyes—into a face identical to his, but darker, colder, as if the reflection was a version of him that he'd never wanted to confront. He stepped back, his pulse pounded in his ears. Was this real? There was no mirror. There couldn't be. The figure standing in front of him was real—or at least, it felt real. He just stared at this person in front of him.

The reflection spoke. "Are you going to leave our mother behind? If you leave now, you'll never be able to see her again. This is what you have always wanted: To be with our mom again. You can't leave."

Steve looked back at his mom, playing with baby Steve.

How could he leave his mom when just got her back?

He started walking towards her mom again but something stopped him. This was not right. His mom was dead. This was just a memory. He had to get out of here. He pictured Charlie, alone, waiting for him to return. Steve had always been there for him, always put him first. But now... now he could have something for himself. Couldn't he? He was convinced for one moment that he should choose his mother but his conscience tugged at him. He couldn't abandon Charlie. He can't be selfish. He had to find the girl and go back to his brother. He again turned towards the door. His reflection was still standing looking at him accusingly.

"Charlie is not your responsibility. He'll be fine on his own. He can take care of himself but you won't get your mother again. This is your only chance. For once, choose yourself. You've always sacrificed yourself for him. Look at her, Steve. She's right there, waiting for you. You can feel her love again—don't you deserve that? All you have to do is stay. Charlie doesn't need you the way she does. This is your one chance to be happy."

These words stirred something in him. Steve's eyes narrowed. This person, whoever he is, can't be his friend. No one who truly cared about him would ever ask him to abandon Charlie. His reflection's words rang hollow, twisted by selfishness. Steve's jaw tightened as he reached for the door. He wasn't that person. He wouldn't leave his brother behind—not for a memory. He can't stay here anymore. He had to leave. Ignoring the continuous warnings given by his reflection, he reached the door and opened it.

Once he was out in the corridor, Steve glanced at the other doors, wondering if they all held fragments of his past.

As Steve walked past the rows of doors, a low murmur seemed to vibrate from one of them.

He paused, glancing at the door, but it was quiet now. A shiver ran down his spine. Was it his imagination?

He moved on, but the sense of unease lingered.

He approached another door, his heart pounding with hope that this one would contain another memory of his mother.

The thought of seeing his mother's gentle face again made his chest tighten with longing. His hand trembled as he reached for the knob. But when the door swung open, his breath caught in his throat. Instead of the warm glow of a familiar memory, the room was filled with swirling grey clouds. A violent storm howled around him, threatening to tear everything apart. The cold wind bit at his skin, the roar of crashing waves drowning out all other sound. Steve stood frozen in the doorway, his mind struggling to make sense of what he saw.

In the middle of the raging ocean, Charlie was fighting against the waves, barely keeping his head above water. Steve's heart lurched. What was Charlie doing here? He'd never been near an ocean in his life. This couldn't be real. Was it even a memory? Charlie's eyes locked onto Steve's, wide with terror. 'Steve! Help me!' His voice was desperate, raw. Steve stood rooted to the spot, unable to move.

How could Charlie see him? This wasn't supposed to happen. Panic gripped Steve as his mind raced with questions, but his feet refused to budge.

Was this really Charlie? Or was it some twisted reflection of something else—something Steve wasn't ready to face? The wind howled louder, the storm growing with every step Steve took toward the ocean's edge.

He could feel the tempest within him, swirling with the same force as the storm. It had been there all along, this anger, this guilt—buried deep but never forgotten. The storm wasn't just outside; it was inside him, too.

Charlie's voice echoed over the crashing waves as Steve's steps faltered. He had failed him once before—hadn't he? Now, as the ocean threatened to swallow Charlie whole, the weight of that failure returned, heavy and suffocating.

This wasn't a memory; it was a reminder. A reminder of what he had tried so hard to forget. He was 10 years old.

He had taken 5year Charlie into the forest to look for rabbits. Their parents had warned him to stay away from the forest, especially at night but that evening their parents were at the market.

Steve had always felt left out.

His friends used to brag about the adventures in the forest, but beneath their tales lay warnings he had ignored. Shadows danced among the trees, whispering of secrets best left untouched. He had wanted to explore, to feel brave, but the forest was a labyrinth, and it would ensnare him—just like his memories.

That evening he had decided to go. He couldn't leave his brother behind. So, he took him along. Soon after entering, he had lost sense of direction and got lost in trees. Charlie was crying wanting to go home. Steve made Charlie sit under a tree while he looked around.

He had finally found the way out. Just when he turned around to get Charlie, he heard a deep, menacing roar from the darkness. It sent chills down his spine, instinctively urging him to flee. He ran from there towards his house leaving Charlie alone in the jungle.

He didn't stop till he was near his house. Luckily, a hunter was roaming the forest at the same time. He had heard Charlie crying and rescued him. That night, he had learned a terrible lesson about fear.

It would linger in his mind, a shadow that crept into every choice he made thereafter. Steve never mentioned this episode to his parents but he never forgave himself for it.

And now, in front of him was Charlie, about to drown. He had to save him this time.

As he intended to move forward, his reflection that he had seen in the previous memory surfaced before him shimmering ominously in the turbulent water, it's voice lilting and mocking.

"Trying to save your little brother, are we now?" Steve ignored these words. "You think you can change the past? How quaint. Go ahead, dive in— see what becomes of you both."

"Could you just get out of my face!" but the reflection was not to be deterred.

"A shadow trying to chase a ghost. What a fool you've become." it murmured, its voice threading through the crashing waves. "Dive in, and you'll sink like you always have—into nothingness."

His heart raced, caught between the instinct to save Charlie and the chilling voice of reason echoing in his mind.

Sacrifice had always been his burden—whether it was abandoning Charlie that night or sacrificing his dreams for the sake of others.

Steve's breath came in short, ragged gasps as the reflection's words tightened around his heart. The water churned, beckoning him forward, but something rooted him to the spot. Then, Charlie's voice broke through the chaos. 'Steve... please..." When Steve heard those words, it didn't matter to him that it wasn't real, it didn't matter that he would risk his life. All that mattered was he couldn't leave him in the hands of death again! He would never be able to come out of this guilt. He spotted a small boat in the corner, half-hidden beneath the shadows. Without thinking, he ran toward it, shoving it into the violent waters. The moment he paddled into the waves; the world shifted. The cold hit him first—sharp and unforgiving, like a thousand needles piercing his skin. Then, the blackness swarmed in, suffocating him, dragging him under until there was nothing but the void.

CHAPTER FIVE

LUCAS

Steve's head pounded as he opened his eyes, the throbbing pain making it hard to focus. His last memory was of the boat—paddling into the deadly waters, and then... nothing. Now, he found himself in an unfamiliar room, the air heavy with the scent of damp wood and dust. Shelves lined the walls, each one stuffed with items he couldn't quite make out in the dim light. Where the hell was he?

"You're awake, finally!" A man's voice echoed from a shadowed corner.

Steve jerked his head toward the sound, wincing as pain shot through his skull. Slowly, the man emerged from the darkness, striding toward him with unnerving confidence. He sat down, a hint of amusement playing across his face.

"Who... who are you?" Steve managed, his voice thick with pain and confusion.

The man smiled, extending his hand. "I'm Lucas."

The man had American accent. Steve hesitated, eyeing the stranger's outstretched hand warily.

He wasn't sure if he wanted to trust him, but out of instinct—or maybe just politeness—he took it. Lucas was about his age. He had black hair and warm smile. Lucas' clothes, though neat, looked like something from a history book—worn leather boots and a shirt with faded embroidery. Steve blinked, unsure if the man had wandered off the set of an old movie or if something more sinister was at play. Lucas continued to gaze at Steve in amazement as if he had not seen another human in a long time. Steve just blinked at him. He was still feeling very disoriented from the whole ordeal.

"How long have I been out?"

Lucas' smile widened as if Steve had asked the most amusing question.

"How long? I don't know, may be a couple of hours. It's hard to tell. I stopped keeping track of time long back. Watches don't work and the sun is always about to set but never does."

"Sun? what sun? I can only see darkness everywhere."

Lucas raised an eyebrow, amused. "Interesting," he murmured, a small smile tugging at his lips.

"You can't see it? It's always there, just on the horizon. Always about to set, but never quite does. Odd that you can't feel it."

The disorientation from earlier only deepened.

"You're saying there's sunlight? But... how?"

He ran a hand through his hair, the tension mounting in his voice.

"I've been walking in complete darkness. Are we even seeing the same place?"

Lucas shrugged, seemingly unfazed. "Maybe the sun's not for everyone to see."

Steve had more pressing issues to think about.

"Where am I? And... what is this place?" Steve's voice was tight with urgency.

"Oh, this is a library, the only place where humans can exist comfortably," Lucas said, his tone so nonchalant it felt unsettling. "And yeah, found you lying unconscious in the corridor of the tricky house—funny place, that one."

"Tricky house?", Steve's voice was barely above a whisper.

"Well, yeah," Lucas replied with a soft chuckle. "I've named each building around here based on what it does.

There's also the Spinning Hall, the Endlessly Collapsing Bridge—oh, and the place I call The Maze of Insufferable Silence. Great place for meditation, if you're into that sort of thing. Not much else to do when you've got a thousand years to kill."

He grinned to himself, clearly amused by his own words. Steve's mind flashed back to what the strange man had said earlier—someone wandering for a thousand years. Lucas... could it be him? His stomach knotted, the unease creeping up his spine.

"Good thing I get bored and wander through these buildings every so often. Who knows how long you'd have been there otherwise," His words were light, almost indifferent, like it was just another part of his strange, endless routine.

Lucas walked towards a table, opened a drawer and took something out of it.

He gave it to Steve and said, "Eat. You look haggard from all the hunger."

Steve looked at the food. It looked like a fruit but didn't quite recognize it.

He brought it closer to his face, the skin felt rubbery, and its faint scent didn't help calm his nerves. He was not sure if he should eat it, that too given by a stranger, who can be a friend or foe. He kept looking at it suspiciously and yet his mouth started watering and he was almost sure Lucas could hear the rumbling in his stomach.

"It's snakehead. It's doesn't taste much but helps you keep alive."

"Snakehead!!???"

"O, just another of my quirky names.", he said looking quite satisfied with himself. "It's the only edible thing you find around here. I found that out the hard way!!", Lucas chuckled.

His smile was wide, but his eyes held something—Steve couldn't tell if it was amusement or calculation.

Steve stared at the food. He had no choice. He was hungry and he didn't know how long he could survive without food.

His stomach growled, louder this time, almost pleading. Desperation was stronger than fear. He had to take the chance. He took a bite. It was as if his tongue flooded with all the tastes at once.

It was sour, sweet, bitter, spicy and salty – all at once. He wanted to puke. It wasn't just the taste—it felt like his mouth was on fire, then ice. His stomach churned, and for a moment, he wondered if it would betray him completely.

"You sure this isn't poison?" he muttered, wiping his mouth.

He swallowed it somehow and took another bite.

He asked casually, "How did you end up here?"

"It's a long story. Wanted to do something big in life. Read about this mysterious train that takes you to strange places. I wanted adventure. It was difficult to find that damn train. I spent years chasing stories, every dead-end pulling me deeper into obsession. And then, one day, I found it. I didn't even believe it at first—a train, just like they said, but there was something...off. Once I stepped on, I knew there was no going back. And now...well, here I am.", Lucas ended the story with a sad smile and for the first time

Steve felt like believing him.

"Why didn't you try to escape?" Steve asked, taking another reluctant bite of whatever horror that was.

His stomach still churned from the flood of flavours, but hunger clawed at him more fiercely.

"I did. For a long time, I tried everything I could think of but got nothing except sneers from those souls protecting the memories. Then, I resigned. There's no way out." His last words landed heavily, like a final nail in a coffin.

They weren't just words; they were a sentence—a verdict.

"Hold on," Steve said, wiping his mouth and narrowing his eyes at Lucas. "Why did you call the men protecting the memories souls?"

Lucas looked at him, almost pityingly. "You don't know?"

His voice lowered, as if revealing a secret too dangerous to speak aloud. "They look human, but they're not. Just souls. Empty, floating memories stuck in this place. You can't touch them. And they can appear and disappear whenever they want."

He shuddered slightly, as though recalling an encounter too haunting to forget.

Steve's pulse quickened. Souls? This place was beyond anything he'd ever imagined.

His grip tightened on the food, now feeling more like a sick joke.

If Lucas was right, Steve wasn't just trapped—he was at the mercy of ghosts, untouchable beings who could bend reality itself. Before Steve could process this, Lucas reached into his coat and handed him what looked like an old, rusted bottle. The glass was cloudy, as if it hadn't been opened in years.

"Drink," Lucas said in a tone so casual it sent a chill through Steve. "You'll feel dizzy for a while, but you'll survive."

Steve didn't move. He just stared at Lucas, struggling to make sense of the strange man standing before him. Everything about Lucas seemed both unsettling and calm—too calm for someone trapped in a place where souls guarded memories. Steve's mind raced. Could he trust him? The food, the drink—was this all part of some twisted game, or was Lucas genuinely trying to help?

As he took the bottle from him, he finally found his voice.

"Dizzy, you say?"

The bottle felt heavier than it looked, the liquid inside sloshing sluggishly as Steve held it. His throat tightened at the thought of taking a sip, but hunger and survival instincts fought against his fear.

Was he really ready to gamble his life on the words of a man he barely knew? Lucas smiled—a faint, unsettling curve of his lips.

"It's better than the alternative."

Steve didn't even want to know what the alternative was. Suddenly, a sharp memory jolted him—Charlie. The image of him drowning flashed in Steve's mind, his face disappearing beneath the dark water. Panic clawed at his chest. I need to go back, he thought. I left him. I have to save him.

"I need to go back. My brother, Charlie, he's drowning."

Lucas shook his head with a grim smile.

"Don't even think about it. Charlie's not real."

Steve's eyes widened. "What do you mean? I saw him—he was drowning!"

Lucas leaned in, his voice low and steady, as though explaining something he'd said a thousand times.

"It's just a manifestation of your inner fears. If you go back, you'll just black out again. The place twists your mind, Steve. Trust me, Charlie's gone."

CHAPTER SIX

THE FIRST CLUE

"You didn't tell me why you came here?" Lucas asked.

Steve hesitated. Should he tell Lucas everything? The thought of what he might lose lingered, heavy, at the back of his mind. He managed to give a brief account of all the events that happened until before meeting him.

"A memory in exchange of a memory!!" exclaimed Lucas in a voice similar to a child seeing his favourite toy in a shop. "That's crazy. You can't do that. What if you forget me? Lucas chuckled, but there was a flicker of unease in his eyes. "I'll have to give my introduction all over again. Just imagine that!"

Steve forced a smile, but his mind churned. Lucas's carefree laugh felt out of place in this strange, dangerous world.

"I'll find a way to get out of here but first I need to find that girl. Maybe she's the key to escaping this nightmare." Steve said these words more to himself than to Lucas.

The dim light flickered as Steve dwelled on these thoughts, the walls around them almost seeming to pulse with the weight of forgotten memories. He got up to go meet that soul protecting the memories. Lucas tagged along.

"I won't miss this for anything," Lucas had grinned, though there was a glint of something more—something unreadable—behind his smile.

They reached the place where first Steve had met that soul. There was no one in sight.

"Do you know where we can find them?" Steve asked Lucas but before he could answer, a voice echoed through the space, low and eerie.

"Looking for me?"

The words seemed to ripple through the air, chilling them both as they turned to see the soul standing before them. He looked different from before. He no longer looked human.

His form had twisted, shadows swirling around him like dark tendrils, and his eyes gleamed with a malevolent light.

His clothes were now black as night and in his hand, a gnarled staff that seemed to hum with danger.

Steve's heart raced as he stared at the transformed figure. This wasn't the soul he had met before—it was something darker, more dangerous. He could feel a knot tightening in his stomach as he realized they were no longer safe.

"Ready to trade memories?", asked the soul in a deep voice.

"You had said that there's no way out of here then why do you want to help me find the girl? What difference does it make to you?", Steve tried to sound brave.

"Let's just say I have my reasons.", the soul's smile twisted into something darker, its eyes gleaming with a hunger Steve couldn't fully understand. "So, which memory do you want to give up in exchange of the first clue?"

Steve had already thought about this. In the 29 years of his life, he had lot of memories that had no emotional significance and were of trivial importance.

As if reading his mind the soul said, "The memory has to be one which has emotional significance to you, otherwise the deal is off."

Steve felt a sense of helplessness gripping him at hearing these words.

Which memory is he ready to part with? Every memory meant something to him, it was a part of him. How could he just give it away?

"I don't have eternity to wait. Decide fast." Urged the soul.

Steve's mind raced, his thoughts tangled in a knot of fear and confusion. Each memory flashed before him like snapshots, pulling at his heart. He thought of the time when he had mastered to learn his first bike. He was five. The memory of learning to ride a bike as a child wasn't just a milestone—it was the first time he had conquered fear, the first time he felt in control of his life. Letting go of it felt like tearing away a piece of his soul. His first victory on the bike, his mother's proud smile—could he really part with that? The soul's lips curled upward as if it had plucked the thought straight from Steve's mind.

"Ah, yes, your first victory,' it sneered. "So pure, so untainted. Perfect."

"How am I supposed to give my memory?"

"Just close your eyes and concentrate on the memory you want to give. After a point, you won't remember it anymore."

Steve closed his eyes, with heavy heart, he remembered riding the bike perfectly for the first time. The excitement overtaking him, the slaps he got on back from his dad and the kisses he got from his mother. As the memory slipped away, a strange numbness spread through Steve's chest. The warmth of his father's slaps on his back, the soft brush of his mother's kisses—they faded like mist in the morning sun. And then, a cold emptiness filled the space where the memory had lived, a hollow ache that throbbed in his heart. When Steve opened his eyes, a long, polished table materialized out of the shadows, its surface lined with countless glass jars. The air around them shimmered, as if each jar held something fragile and alive. One jar lifted from its place, hovering midair, glowing faintly like it was beckoning to him.

The soul pointed towards the jar and said, "That's your first clue. Take it."

"Wait, I thought I could choose which memory I want."

"You don't choose memories, they choose you. They know exactly what you need."

Steve's hands shook as they reached for the jar, the weight of what he had lost pressing on him like a dark cloud. He didn't know why, but he felt as though his entire life hinged on what was inside, as though letting it go might unravel him completely.

An hourglass appeared on their right, its sand shimmering with a faint, unnatural glow. Steve's heart skipped a beat as the soul's sinister voice slithered into his ears, "As soon as you enter the memory, the sand will start to fall. Fail to find the clue before the last grain slips through, and you'll be trapped in it... forever."

The final word hung in the air, heavy and sharp, like a guillotine blade poised to drop. As they walked back to the library, Steve held the jar close, its weight far heavier than its small size.

He could feel the loss of his memory gnawing at him, an emptiness that made him want to cradle the jar like a lifeline, desperate not to let go. Once inside, Steve opened the jar with trembling hands.

The jar clicked open with a soft hiss, and at once, thick steam gushed out, swirling around them like mist in the dead of night.

The air turned hot and damp, the scent of something ancient and forgotten filling their lungs. Steve squeezed his eyes shut as the steam pricked at his skin, leaving behind a cold sweat. When it finally cleared, there was a door in front of them. They both looked at the door and then at each other with open mouths. Steve took a deep breath and started walking toward the door. Lucas started walking with him. Steve stopped.

"Where do you think you're going?" Steve asked, narrowing his eyes at Lucas, who was already at his side.

"I'm not staying here alone, mate," Lucas replied, puffing out his chest with exaggerated pride.

"We don't know what dangers lay ahead. For all we know, we could be trapped inside forever."

"Dangers or not, I'm not letting you hog all the glory."

Steve rolled his eyes. "Or the disaster."

"Hey, I help my comrades," Lucas said, mock indignation flashing across his face. "Can't leave you in there to face the unknown on your own."

Steve sighed, knowing better than to argue, and together, they went toward the door.

It loomed ahead, dark and foreboding. As Steve's hand hovered over the knob, a sudden cold crept up his spine, a silent warning that whatever lay beyond this door wasn't just dangerous—it was something far worse. As he opened the door, they entered a dimly lit, abandoned warehouse filled with shadows and echoes of struggle. The warehouse stretched out before them like a cavern of shadows, the air thick with the scent of damp concrete and rusted metal.

Faint, flickering lights cast long, menacing shadows on the walls, amplifying the sounds of distant scuffling and low, guttural grunts. Every step echoed ominously, as if the place itself was holding its breath. As they step further in, they saw a man tied up and surrounded by a group of menacing figures who were beating him.

The man, battered but alert, caught Steve's eye. "I knew you'd come, Jeffery! You have to listen – don't tell these goons about them. They'll kill them if you do!"

Steve's heart skipped a beat, not out of fear but sheer bewilderment. The name meant nothing to him, yet it stuck.

Why was this man calling him by that name?

But he knew this was not the time to think. He and Lucas ran to help the man. The goons turned as one, their eyes gleaming with malice, their fists tightening around crude weapons. One of them, a hulking figure with scars running down his arms, stepped forward, his voice a low growl.

"Tell us where they are, and maybe we won't turn you into pulp. Your old friend here's been real uncooperative." He grinned, showing a row of broken teeth. Steve had no idea what they were talking about.

Before Steve could process the situation, Lucas stepped forward, his chest puffed out with an exaggerated swagger.

"You think we're scared of you?" Lucas's voice rang out, defiant and wild. "I've taken down better men than you without breaking a sweat."

Steve's stomach twisted. This was the last thing he wanted—a fight, when they were already in over their heads.

He shot a warning glance at Lucas, his mind screaming for caution, but it was too late.

Steve's heart pounded in his chest, a frantic drumbeat urging him to run, to fight, to do anything but stand there frozen.

He wasn't Jeffery. He didn't know who 'they' are. But this man—this stranger—was counting on him. His eyes darted to Lucas, who seemed ready to charge headfirst into danger, and Steve's gut twisted with dread. How had it all gone so wrong so quickly?

Steve looked up at the giant hourglass, its sands falling relentlessly, a constant reminder that time was running out. His heart pounded in his chest, but he swallowed his fear, focusing on the five men standing before him. Their shadows stretched across the warehouse floor, towering like a death sentence waiting to be executed.

"We can talk this out in a peaceful manner," Steve said, his voice cracking as the dryness in his throat grew unbearable. "I know where the they are. I'll tell you, but you need to leave that man alone." The man tied up on the floor shook his head wildly.

"No, don't tell them, Jeffery! It's okay if I die, but I'll never forgive myself if anything happens to them." His voice was strained with fear and desperation, his eyes pleading.

Steve forced himself to ignore the man's panic.

His priority was getting the man out of harm's way first; he'd figure out an escape later.

"Leave him, and I'll give you the information you want," he repeated, forcing more confidence into his voice than he felt. Lucas, who had been watching quietly, gave Steve a blank look but quickly caught on.

"Yes," Lucas chimed in, puffing his chest out. "You think we're bluffing about them just to save him? We know exactly where they are. Let the man go."

Steve shot him a sharp look. This wasn't part of the plan—Lucas was pushing the stakes too far. This was a delicate balance—they were playing for time, but the hourglass wasn't waiting for them. The air was thick with tension. As the goons agreed, a subtle shift in the air sent a chill down Steve's spine. He barely had time to react before he and Lucas were yanked backward, their bodies pulled through the air like puppets on invisible strings. They landed hard at the warehouse entrance—exactly where they'd started. The goons, the man, it was all happening again. The same scene. The same nightmare.

Steve's mind raced, struggling to make sense of what was happening. He glanced at Lucas, who muttered something under his breath. Was this some sort of loop? A test? His heart pounded—there wasn't time to think, only to act. As they rushed toward the warehouse again, a sense of déjà vu overwhelmed Steve. But this time, something was different—an eerie, unnatural silence hung in the air. The goons' blows landed harder, more viciously. And when the man spoke, it was as if he was seeing Steve for the first time again.

"Why is it happening again?" Lucas muttered; his voice edged with frustration.

Steve didn't answer—he was too busy searching the scene for anything, any sign, that might explain this horrifying loop. Time was slipping away, but he felt like they were missing something crucial.

This time, before Steve could respond to the goons, "I don't know who this man is or who 'they' are, and I'm not Jeffery!" Lucas blurted, his voice cracking. "We didn't mean to come here—it was a mistake! We're leaving."

Before Steve could respond, Lucas grabbed his hand and turned to leave.

Steve shot him a look of disbelief. What the hell is he doing? But before he could think of anything else, Once again, they were jerked through the air, landing with a thud at the warehouse entrance. Steve clenched his fists, anger flaring inside him. Lucas had ruined their chance, and time was slipping through their fingers.

"What were you thinking?" Steve snapped as they rushed back toward the warehouse. "We're running out of time, and you just blew it!"

"I was trying to save our necks!" Lucas shot back; his voice defensive but laced with an attempt at humour. "You know I'm brave—I was just... thinking on my feet."

Steve shot him a sideways glance, frustration still simmering. "If you want to help, you need to listen to me. Stop thinking on your feet and start thinking with your head. This isn't going to stop until we figure it out. And if we don't..." His voice dropped, eyes narrowing. "We're dead."

They tried everything—reasoning with the goons, distracting them, attacking from different angles. But every time, they were yanked back to the door, the loop resetting. No matter what they did, the scene played out the same way, like a twisted game they couldn't win. With every failed attempt, the pressure mounted. Time was slipping away.

Frustration gnawed at Steve as he stood at the entrance again, staring at the warehouse. There had to be something they were missing. The man's voice echoed in his mind: "I knew you'd come, Jeffery!" But Steve wasn't Jeffery. Then who was? Why hadn't Jeffery come? His eyes drifted to the hourglass—only a small amount of sand was left, spilling through faster by the second. Suddenly, it clicked.

"We're going about this all wrong," Steve muttered, his heart racing.

He turned to Lucas. "Come on."

Without waiting for an answer, Steve bolted outside, Lucas stumbling after him.

"Why are we running outside? We're supposed to solve the puzzle—save the man!" Lucas called, breathless.

"No, think about it," Steve shot back. "We've tried everything. We even untied the man once and still failed. The problem isn't saving him. The problem is that Jeffery's supposed to be here—and he's not." Lucas slowed, realization hitting him like a wave.

"You're smarter than you look, Steve," he said, a flicker of admiration in his voice.

Trees loomed on every side, swallowing the warehouse in shadow. Steve and Lucas stood still for a moment, unsure which way to turn.

The air was thick with the scent of damp earth and something else—something sour and metallic. Just as they were deciding what to do next, a muffled cry for help cut through the night. They sprinted toward the sound, their breath ragged. The trees twisted together overhead, blocking any trace of moonlight.

Steve stumbled on a root but regained his balance just as they reached a man lying on the ground, bound and gagged. His movements were frantic, struggling against the ropes.

They rushed to help him, freeing him quickly.

The man, once loose, bolted without a word. His feet slapped against the dirt, disappearing into the dark toward the warehouse. Steve watched him go, frowning. He looked oddly familiar. Then, something small glinted in the dim light where the man had been. He knelt and picked it up—a locket, cool and smooth in his palm, with a faintly engraved

"L" on its surface. Steve's heart quickened. He turned to Lucas to say something, but before the words could leave his mouth, the landscape around them began to swirl. Colours and shapes twisted together, disorienting him completely. Then, just as suddenly, the world righted itself. They were standing in the library again, the same silence and dusty air greeting them. Steve opened his hand—the locket was still there, resting cold in his palm. Lucas peered over Steve's shoulder at the locket.

"Fancy trinket for a guy who was running for his life, don't you think? Seems important."

CHAPTER SEVEN

THE WEDDING

As Steve and Lucas searched for the soul to get the second clue, Steve's mind spun with unanswered questions. *What was hidden in that memory? What was I supposed to learn? Was it even a clue or just another twisted joke?* And then there was the man who'd sprinted towards the warehouse. His face—*why did it feel so familiar?* Could he be... *Jeffery?* Before Steve could untangle his thoughts, a low, sinister voice echoed through the space, dripping with malice.

"So, you made it out of the memory, did you? Impressive... I didn't think you had it in you."

Steve and Lucas spun toward the source of the voice, shadows curling in the dim light. The soul's presence felt heavier this time, like the air itself thickened with its arrival. Frustration boiled over in Steve.

"How was that memory supposed to help me?" His voice trembled as it rose. "I didn't learn *anything* about the girl I'm supposed to find!"

The soul's hollow laughter rattled through the room.

"That's for you to figure out, if you're clever enough."

Steve clenched his fists, teeth gritted. Every answer felt just out of reach, taunting him. Lucas, standing beside him, crossed his arms and leaned in with a smirk.

"Yes, and your job is to annoy us, isn't it?" His tone was biting, eyes narrowing as he shot the soul a mocking glance.

The soul hissed, its form flickering slightly, as if Lucas's jab had struck a nerve.

"Careful, boy. You may not like where this path leads."

Steve shot Lucas an impatient look, his frustration mounting. This was no time for pointless jabs.

"What's the second clue?" he demanded; his voice tight.

"Where's the second memory?" The soul's silence was deafening, and the weight of its presence pressed down on Steve.

Helplessness gnawed at him—he wasn't ready to part with another piece of his life. Not yet. But he knew deep down, it was the only way out. Before he could fully process the decision, Lucas chimed in, a burst of enthusiasm that felt out of place in the oppressive atmosphere.

"Hey, take my memory instead. I've got plenty of emotional baggage to throw around."

The soul's cold gaze didn't waver. "No," it replied smoothly, almost relishing the moment. "This is Steve's mission. I'll only take *his* memories."

Lucas's grin faltered, his bravado dimming as he sank back, half crestfallen. Steve swallowed hard, a bitter knot forming in his throat. There was no escaping it. He had to give up more of himself to move forward. The thought left him feeling hollow, as if the memories slipping away were pulling pieces of him with them.

Finally, Steve made his choice: the memory of his 10th birthday. His family had surprised him with his favourite handmade cake, the kind only his mom could bake just right, and the toy he had dreamed of for months. He never knew how his parents managed to pay for it, but back then, he was too happy to care. As the memory of his childhood birthday drifted away, Steve felt a subtle hollowness, like the space left by a missing tooth.

He knew something sweet had once been there, but now, there was only a dull absence. His chest tightened, and without understanding why, tears welled up and rolled down his cheeks.

He wiped them away, knowing something precious had been lost but unable to remember exactly what. In the dim light, the table of jars appeared once again.

One rose into the air, glowing faintly. His second clue. Steve and Lucas exchanged a glance and, without a word, made their way back to the library.

As they walked, Steve broke the silence.

"I really appreciate it, you know... that you were ready to give up your memories for me. Thank you."

Lucas waved it off, flashing a grin. "Oh, it's nothing! I always help a friend in need."

He tipped an imaginary hat and gave a dramatic, sweeping bow. Steve chuckled despite himself. Lucas's antics never failed to lift the mood.

"So, what memories would you have given up if the soul had agreed?"

Lucas straightened, pretending to think hard.

"Well, there's the time I made my first sandwich, the time I took down a hundred men all by myself, and of course, when I starred as the world's finest clown in a street play."

Steve raised an eyebrow, smirking.

"You're always going on about taking down men. Were you some kind of soldier or something?"

Lucas threw back his head and laughed, a sound that echoed through the empty halls as they entered the library.

"A soldier? Nah, I just had a lot of siblings to wrestle with growing up. And for the record, I always won," he added, puffing out his chest proudly.

Steve smiled, feeling lighter for the first time in a while. Lucas had a way of making everything seem a little less impossible. As if in response to his mood, the darkness that had clung to the environment began to recede. The oppressive blackness faded, giving way to soft, muted light that danced along the edges of the walls. Shadows lifted, and the air itself seemed to grow warmer.

"Did you see that?" Steve exclaimed, his eyes widening.

"See what?" Lucas asked, unfazed.

"The darkness... it's gone. There's a faint light instead."

Lucas grinned, casually shrugging. "Well, for me, it's always the sunshine, but looks like you're finally letting in some light, huh?"

Steve paused, mulling over Lucas's words. His gaze drifted to the jar in his hands. The flicker of warmth he had felt moments ago was quickly replaced by a rush of anxiety. His thoughts raced, anticipating what dangers lay ahead. The brief reprieve vanished, and just as quickly as the light had come, the darkness crept back, swallowing the room once more.

The air turned heavy, and Steve's heart sank as he realized the connection between his mood and the environment—it shifted with his emotions, reflecting the turmoil within. He wanted to reflect on it, to understand how deeply this place was tied to his psyche, but there wasn't time.

They had bigger concerns. With a slow, deliberate breath, Steve turned his attention to the jar. His hands trembled slightly as he unscrewed the lid.

As before, a thick fog poured out, swirling around them.

The cold mist clung to their skin, making Steve's heart race, but when it cleared, a new door stood before them, looming and mysterious, waiting to be opened.

With trembling hands, they slowly pushed the door open. On the other side, they found themselves stepping into an unexpected scene—a celebration. The stark contrast from the oppressive darkness caught them off guard. Laughter and music filled the air, mingling with the soft hum of chatter.

People were gathered in clusters, some dancing in the open space, others seated in rows of neatly arranged chairs.

The sweet, intoxicating scent of flowers was overwhelming, their vibrant colours draped everywhere, as if the entire scene had been drenched in petals.

Steve glanced around, trying to make sense of it. In the centre stood an empty stage, adorned with garlands and flickering lights.

It looked like a wedding was about to begin, but there was no bride or groom in sight.

They moved forward cautiously, the joy around them feeling surreal, almost unnerving in contrast to their grim purpose.

Steve's eyes darted from face to face—each person appeared real, yet something felt *off*. He couldn't shake the sense that beneath the smiles and celebration, something was hiding.

A man from the crowd approached them and addressed Steve, "Hey Jeff, how come you're here? We thought you were in the city with your girl."

His eyes flicked over to Lucas with a touch of suspicion.

"Who's this man? Never seen him around."

Steve's mind raced—Jeff had to mean Jeffery. He knew the smart move was to play along.

"Hi, she wanted to spend time with her friend, so I came back. This is Lucas, my friend, from the city." Steve hoped his words made enough sense.

"Now you've even got a girl I don't know about?" Lucas whispered with a smirk, leaning in close.

Steve shot him a quick glance, his voice sharp and low, "Not now. Just follow my lead."

The man turned to the crowd, raising his voice.

"See who's here—it's Jeff!"

In an instant, the crowd erupted with excitement.

People surrounded Steve and Lucas from all sides, their faces lighting up with joy.

"We're so glad you're here!"

"We thought you'd not make it!"

"Will you dance with me?"

"Hey, don't hog him all to yourself!"

The voices came from every direction, each person vying for his attention. Steve felt the buzz of energy, smiles and laughter all around, but it was dizzying—he didn't know where to look or whom to answer first. It was clear that this Jeffery guy, whoever he was, was popular here. Lucas nudged him lightly, grinning.

"Looks like you're the local hero, Jeff."

Steve forced a smile, though his nerves were fraying. "I'm starting to wish I wasn't."

As if the heavens had heard his silent plea, the crowd suddenly shifted their focus as the bride and groom made their entrance. Steve exhaled, relieved to have the spotlight slip away.

The bride, in a stunning white gown, and the groom, sharp in a black suit, walked onto the stage, drawing everyone's attention.

The ceremony began, with vows exchanged and rings slipped onto fingers.

When the groom kissed the bride, a wave of cheers erupted. The joy in the room was palpable, and Steve almost managed to relax—until the bride tossed her bouquet. It arced high through the air, spinning as if it had a mind of its own. And somehow, despite the odds, it landed squarely in Steve's hands. For a second, the room went quiet. Then, chaos. The crowd erupted, going ballistic at the sight.

One of the girls from the crowd stepped forward, smiling shyly. "Would you like to dance?" she asked. Steve hesitated for a moment, but couldn't refuse.

Out of politeness, he agreed. The air was filled with music as they swayed together.

Meanwhile, Lucas had stationed himself by the liquor table, clearly enjoying the atmosphere. Lights twinkled across the dance floor, couples moved to the soothing rhythm, and the scent of delicious food hung in the air. It was the picture of a perfect evening—or so they all thought. After a while, Steve gently excused himself and made his way to Lucas.

"Enjoying the party?" he asked with a half-smile.

"Not as much as you, buddy. Girls asking you to dance and all," Lucas teased, raising his glass in mock celebration.

Steve waved the comment away. "I'm finding this whole celebration unsettling," he said, lowering his voice. "We're supposed to be here for a clue, but there's nothing that suggests anything is wrong. Everyone's too... happy."

Just as he finished speaking, he overheard a conversation nearby between two men.

"Did Michael come yet? He was supposed to leave right after the marriage," one man asked, concern lacing his voice.

"I haven't seen him at all during the celebration," the other replied, sounding worried.

Steve's attention piqued. He approached them cautiously.

"Is something wrong?" he asked.

The men shifted uncomfortably, exchanging nervous glances. One cleared his throat but didn't speak, the other glanced toward the road, as if expecting something—or someone. Steve's curiosity grew.

Something's off, he thought, noticing the way they avoided his question.

It wasn't just Michael's absence; it was the fear simmering beneath their silence, like a secret no one dared voice.

Steve's pulse quickened.

He had a feeling this was the thread they needed to pull, but the men were reluctant to tug.

"We can't find Michael anywhere. Have you seen him around?", one of them finally asked with reluctance and hope reflecting all at once, in his eyes.

Steve paused, unsure of who Michael was. "No," he said, shaking his head. "I haven't seen him anywhere."

The men's worry deepened, and Steve's unease grew. Suddenly, a man came running towards them, panting and his eyes full of fear.

"Michael... he's dead. His body... outside the village," the man gasped, clutching his chest between words, eyes wide with fear.

Somehow, the word spread and everyone was in a state of panic. Everyone, including the bride and the groom, ran in the direction the man was taking them.

His body lay crumpled at the village's edge, blood smeared across his torn clothes, chunks of flesh missing as though something had ripped into him.

A collective gasp rose from the crowd, women shrieked and covered their faces, while others stood frozen, wide-eyed and pale. The groom stumbled back, his hands trembling, and the bride clutched her veil, her knuckles white as she stumbled back in disbelief. Her eyes, wide with horror, darted between the body and her groom, seeking answers that no one could give. Trembling, she covered her mouth as if to stifle a scream, but her silent shock was more haunting than any sound.

"We should have done more to stop him," a man murmured, wiping away a tear. "He didn't have to do it alone... maybe if we had insisted, if we hadn't let him go—" He broke off, voice cracking.
"How will we face her now? Her brother was her last family," another whispered, eyes downcast.

"He gave himself for us," someone sobbed, their voice trembling.

Steve and Lucas just stood there, not knowing what to do or what to say.

"Jeff," the bride said quietly, her voice breaking the silence.

"You have to tell her. You're the only one she'll listen to." Her eyes held his, pleading but resolute. "Please. She's lost everything."

Steve's stomach twisted at the thought of it. He didn't know who this girl was, but from the way they spoke of her, he could tell it was no small task.

'Handle her?' How could he when he didn't even know what to say? Yet, he nodded, his heart heavy with guilt he didn't quite understand. He glanced at the hourglass, watching the sand trickle away, its silent ticking a reminder of how little time he had. Every grain that fell was a step closer to failure, to letting Michael's sacrifice mean nothing. He didn't have time to find this girl, let alone console her. Yet, somehow, he knew this was his burden now—the task that Michael had left incomplete.

Steve's mind raced. He wanted to ask what the incomplete task was, but something stopped him—was it because, in their eyes, he was Jeffery? Shouldn't Jeffery already know? If he asked the wrong question, he might reveal too much about himself. Reluctantly, he nudged Lucas to ask instead.

"So," Lucas said, glancing at the man beside him, "what's this dangerous, evil-slaying task Michael was supposed to do? Sounds like quite the heroic mission."

The man sighed; his gaze distant as he began to explain. "New born babies go missing from the village at every full moon night. Since the last decade, people have been living in fear. No one knows who's behind it and where the babies go."

The man's voice faltered, as if he wasn't sure he should continue.

"We've searched everywhere... and found nothing," he whispered. "Some say... spirits. Others...." He swallowed hard, his eyes darting around. "Others think it's someone here... someone we know. Michael thought he could find the truth," the man said, shaking his head. "But now he's dead, and I'm starting to wonder if he got too close to something none of us were meant to know. No one lets their children out of sight anymore," the man said, his eyes darting around nervously. "Everyone's afraid their baby will be next."

The man's voice broke on the last words, a heavy sigh escaping him.

As the man spoke, the wind seemed to pick up, howling faintly through the trees, as if echoing the village's despair. Steve shivered, though it wasn't the cold that unsettled him. He glanced at the villagers. No one met his eyes. They stood huddled together, casting wary glances around, as if any one of them might be the culprit. Lucas raised an eyebrow.

"Missing babies, huh? Sounds like a bad ghost story." But the man's trembling hand and fearful expression told Steve this was no bedtime tale.

Steve intervened hoping he was not asking the wrong question, "How was he planning to proceed with his plan?"

"He was going to be your brother-in-law. If he didn't tell you, what makes you think he'd tell any of us?"

'Brother-in-law?' The words hit Steve like a punch to the gut, a detail he'd never seen coming. How could that be true? He barely had time to question it before... a shadowy figure stepped out from the edge of the crowd, his eyes locking on Steve's.

"Come with me," he whispered, barely audible over the noise around them.

Without waiting for a response, he turned toward the road leading away from the village and strode off into the growing dusk. The figure moved with purpose, his footsteps silent, like a shadow slipping through the cracks of the fading daylight. Steve hesitated, exchanging a wary glance with Lucas. Something felt off, the unease gnawing at the back of his mind. Who was this man, and why did it feel like following him was stepping into the unknown? They gave each other a barely perceptible nod. With no better options, they followed.

Once they reached a secluded spot, the man stopped abruptly and turned toward Steve.

He was tall and thin, his skin pale and stretched tight over sharp cheekbones. His wide, unblinking eyes gave him a haunted look beneath his long black coat, which seemed to absorb the shadows around him, as though he were mourning something lost.

In a soft, almost unnerving voice, he said, "I know you're in this memory looking for clues. I can help you."

Whatever Steve had expected this man to say, it wasn't this. His mouth fell open, words caught in his throat.

Next to him, Lucas' face drained of colour, his breath catching as if he had seen a ghost.

"Wh—what? How do you...?" Steve stammered, struggling to form a coherent question.

"If you go 20 kilometres south from here," the man continued, his tone calm and unaffected by their shock, "you'll reach a mountain. The locals call it the Mountain of Death.

No one who climbs it ever comes back." He paused, his eyes narrowing slightly. "But if you make it to the other side, you'll find the answers you're looking for." With those cryptic words hanging in the air, the man melted into the shadows, leaving behind only an unsettling silence and a lingering sense of foreboding.

Steve and Lucas stood frozen, uncertainty gnawing at them.

The villagers knew nothing of Michael's intentions, and this lead—however dubious—felt like their only option. Sand slipped through the hourglass of time, each grain a reminder of their dwindling chances to uncover the truth.

With reluctance heavy in their steps, they began to follow the man's directions. They trudged through unfamiliar terrain, unsure how long they had been walking before the jagged silhouette of a mountain finally loomed on the horizon. Exhaustion tugged at them, and their throats were parched from the endless journey.

"I think there's a spring over there," Lucas said, his voice cracking with hope as he pointed to a distant spot where birds circled above. "Maybe we can get some water."

Grateful for a moment's respite, they quickened their pace toward the river, which flowed with an eerie serenity. The water shimmered under the fading light, its calm surface belying the unease that tormented him.

But thirst clouded their judgment. Without hesitation, they knelt by the riverbank and took a long, greedy sip.

The world around them shifted instantly. A suffocating blackness swallowed everything in an instant, as if the river itself had poisoned the air.

Before either of them could react, their vision blurred, and the weight of unconsciousness dragged them down.

Their bodies lay still beside the river, vulnerable and unaware of the danger that lurked in the shadows.

When Steve woke up, his head pounded with pain. For a few disoriented moments, his vision blurred, and he struggled to make sense of his surroundings. Slowly, he tried to sit up, every movement intensifying the dizziness that gripped him.

As his eyes began to focus, a chill of realization crept through him—he was surrounded by endless reflections of himself. Panic rose swiftly, tightening his chest.

He got to his feet, stumbling as he shoved at the mirrors, hoping one might give way to a door. None did.

"Lucas?" he called out, voice tinged with desperation.

Silence greeted him, and dread twisted inside him. Where was Lucas? He was the only companion Steve had on this lonely, dangerous journey. For a moment, there was no response. Just when the weight of isolation threatened to close in on him, he heard a faint mumbling. Relief surged through him.

"Lucas!" Steve shouted again. "Can you hear me?"

"Steve? Help! I'm surrounded by... me!" Lucas's voice was frantic, sounding far away but strangely close, like an echo bouncing around the mirrored chamber.

Despite the situation, Steve almost smiled at Lucas's words.

"You're surrounded by mirrors, Lucas," he called out, trying to keep his voice steady, though his own anxiety simmered just below the surface.

"Why can't I see you?" Lucas's voice had an edge of fear.

"I don't know. I'm trying to figure that out," Steve replied, his mind racing.

Their voices sounded as though they were standing next to each other, but their reflections betrayed them, multiplying endlessly, each reflection more disorienting than the last.

As Steve frantically searched for an escape, a cold laugh echoed through the mirrored room, sending a chill down his spine.

He froze, eyes darting from one reflection to the next, trying to locate the source of the sound. Suddenly, in one of the mirrors, a figure materialized—a familiar one.

The man who had led them to this place.

He stood tall, his eyes gleaming with amusement, his dark coat blending into the shadows that seemed to stretch endlessly behind him.

"Enjoying your little puzzle?" the man sneered, his voice dripping with mockery. "I told you, didn't I? I could help you. And yet, here you are—lost, confused, trapped."

Steve's chest tightened with anger as he locked eyes with the reflection.

"You did this on purpose," he growled, fists clenching at his sides. "You tricked us."

The man chuckled softly, his grin widening as he folded his arms. "I just did what I was told, my friend. It's not my fault you were so... eager to follow. After all, you're the one trying to solve this little mystery, aren't you? Should've known better than to trust a stranger so easily."

Steve's heart raced, fury and frustration twisting in his gut.

"Who told you to do this? Who are you working for?"

The man didn't answer directly, only shook his head with a look of exaggerated pity.

"That's for you to figure out—if you ever get out of here alive."

He stepped closer to the glass, his face looming large in the reflection.

"But I wouldn't get your hopes up. No one gets out of the Mirror Room. At least, not without paying the price."

The man's face flickered and shimmered, multiplying across the mirrors, appearing in each one like a ghost taunting them from every direction.

"Good luck finding the way out. You'll need it," he said with a malicious grin before his reflection began to fade, his image dissolving back into the cold, unfeeling glass.

Steve stood motionless; his breath heavy. For a moment, the weight of their situation pressed down on him harder than ever. But then, from the other side of the room, Lucas's voice broke through.

"What...what did he mean by that, Steve? How are we supposed to get out?"

Steve stared at his own reflection, the man's words echoing in his head. He took a deep breath, pushing back the fear rising in his chest.

"We'll find a way, Lucas," he said, more to convince himself than Lucas.

"We've made it this far, haven't we?"

But even as he spoke, the mirrors around him seemed to close in, their cold, mocking reflections daring him to fail.

CHAPTER EIGHT

THE MIRROR ROOM

Steve looked at the reflections around him. Each reflection was different. One showed him as a ten-year-old boy. Another displayed him as a teenager, and yet another presented him as an old man. Only one reflection revealed his true identity, yet it didn't mirror his actions; instead, it offered him a cold stare that sent a shiver down his spine. Just then, he noticed a mirror that didn't have a reflection at all. The emptiness of that glass unnerved him, leaving a pit of dread in his stomach. Standing in front of a mirror and not seeing himself felt like confronting a shadow of his own existence. Confusion and fear swirled within him as he took a step back, grappling with the unsettling nature of the reflections surrounding him. Compelled by a mix of curiosity and trepidation, Steve approached the mirror that portrayed him as a ten-year-old boy.

As he moved closer, the background began to transform, revealing shifting shadows that flickered like candlelight on the walls. The shadows took on vague human forms, mimicking his every movement with an eerie accuracy. Overwhelmed by the uncanny sight, he instinctively recoiled, a chill racing down his spine. With a racing heart, he then turned to the mirror showing his teenage self. The scene shifted again, morphing into a foggy, desolate landscape where trees twisted and writhed as if alive. The air thickened with mist, and he could hear faint whispers echoing around him, words he couldn't quite grasp but that dripped with unease.

Next, he ventured to the mirror where he appeared as an old man. This reflection revealed flames flickering against a dark sky, illuminating shadowy figures huddled around a fire.

Their distorted forms seemed to be locked in a dance of fear and desperation.

Finally, he returned to the mirror displaying his true self, where a still body of water lay beneath him.

It rippled ominously, as if something unseen lurked beneath the surface. He turned his gaze to the mirror devoid of any reflection, where a glimmering key hung in mid-air, suspended as if it were a piece of a larger puzzle. Steve glanced around, his heart pounding; there was no key in sight, only the surreal image taunting him from the glass. He reached out to touch it, but his fingers met only cold, unyielding glass, leaving him to wonder what the key unlocked and why it was so tantalizingly out of reach.

Just then, he heard Lucas's voice cut through the tense silence.

"Steve! Did you think of a way to get out of here?" Panic laced his tone.

"No, not yet. What do you see in the reflections, Lucas?"

Lucas's voice took on a strange urgency. "That's the odd part! All my reflections have suddenly been replaced by yours. I see you as a child, as a teenager, as an old man, and one showing you as you are now."

"What? Why are you seeing my reflections?" Steve asked, bewildered.

"I don't know. It's like you're everywhere, but you're not."

"So, we're seeing the same things? But why?"

"Maybe the room likes you more," Lucas quipped, almost chuckling at his own joke.

Steve rolled his eyes in response. "Or maybe you should just learn where to speak what," he replied, irritation creeping into his voice. "Now, be quiet for a moment and let me think of a way out."

Steve looked at the hourglass. It was already half-empty. If they didn't escape this mirror maze soon, they'd be trapped in this memory forever. Panic surged within him, tightening his chest, but he forced himself to think quickly. His gaze flitted between the eerie reflections staring back at him and the key suspended in mid-air.

The key. His mind raced for a solution. As his dad always used to say, *every problem comes with a solution—you just need to know where to look.* He moved closer to the mirror where the key hung, examining it closely. The shape, the size—none of it seemed out of place, but something about the design on the head of the key tugged at his memory.

Where had he seen it before? He racked his brain, the nagging familiarity of the symbol lingered, an unshakable feeling scratching at his thoughts. Then, it hit him like a punch in the gut—it was the same symbol he'd seen on John's hand. The same John who had come with the proposal to find the girl. A cold shiver crawled down Steve's spine. At the time, he hadn't thought much of it—just an odd mark. But now, seeing it engraved on this key, it felt like more than a coincidence. Could John be connected to this? Why would he have that symbol? The question weighed heavily on his mind as his eyes flicked back to the hourglass, the sand slipping away too quickly.

Absentmindedly, Steve began tracing the symbol on the mirror with his fingers, his mind lost in thought. There had to be a connection— and just as he finished drawing it, a sudden shift occurred. The reflections vanished.

Steve spun around, and beside him, a large square frame materialized, empty but humming with possibility.

On the mirrors, scenes began to flicker to life—shadowy figures, half-formed images, whispers of a story waiting to be told.

The symbol was the key, but Steve still didn't understand *how*.

He glanced between the mirrors, realizing the pieces of the puzzle were scattered, waiting for him to put them in the right order—if he could figure it out in time

"Lucas, do you notice anything different?" Steve asked, his voice tight with concern over Lucas' uncharacteristic silence.

"Yes, Steve! There are scenes playing on each mirror now, but they're incomplete ... like fragments," Lucas replied, his voice echoing from the distance.

"I see them too," Steve said, eyeing the shifting images. "It's like we're supposed to put the pieces together, like a puzzle."
"But what about this empty square?" Lucas asked, pointing at the hollow frame.

"I'm not sure... maybe it's where the puzzle fits together." Steve felt the weight of time pressing against him as he examined each mirror more closely, urgency creeping into his every movement.

One mirror showed a baby caught in the swift current of a river, drifting helplessly. Another showed a group of men running, their faces obscured in shadow. In another, flames engulfed a woman, her body writhing as her agonizing screams filled the air, the sound sending chills through Steve.

Questions swirled in Steve's mind: Were the men running to save the woman and the baby? Did she set herself on fire, or was something far darker at play?

And why was the baby floating down the river? Was it hers? His chest tightened as the puzzle pieces swirled in a storm of confusion—each fragment incomplete, yet disturbingly connected.

In the fourth mirror, one of the men was holding the baby. Had they rescued it from the water? In another reflection, a group of people were gathered around a large tree, their heads bowed in prayer.

Were they mourning the woman who burned? Or were they the ones responsible? Then, another mirror showed a quiet, deserted village, smoke rising from the chimneys, but no sign of life anywhere.

What story were these broken fragments trying to tell him? His mind raced. The scenes felt like pieces of a jigsaw puzzle—disjointed, twisted, and wrong.

"Lucas, what do you think the story is about?" Steve asked, desperation creeping into his voice.

"Maybe it's a nightmare a boy has over and over," Lucas replied, his voice trembling slightly, betraying the fear he was trying to mask.

Steve sighed. "Yeah, that's really helpful. Thanks," he muttered sarcastically, frustration bubbling beneath the surface as he kept trying to make sense of it all.

He touched the scene where the woman was burning, he was able to hold it in his hand like a card, the fragment playing over and over. Carefully, he took it to the square and placed it in the upper left corner, where it loomed ominously. Next, he returned for the piece with the baby floating on the water, positioning it beside the first one. Then he added the piece with the men running, followed by the one depicting a man holding a baby.

Finally, he placed the scene of people praying in front of the tree, leaving the deserted village for last.

With the square now complete, Steve braced himself, expecting something—anything—to happen that would aid their escape.

But nothing occurred. The scenes merely stared back at him, and he felt an unsettling sense of mockery in their stillness. Confusion washed over him.

He had arranged the pieces according to what he thought was the sequence of events: the woman burning, leaving the baby alone; the men rushing to help; the rescue of the baby; the mourning for the woman; and finally, the quiet aftermath.

Where had he gone wrong? Was the sequence incorrect? It felt as if the answer was right in front of him, just out of reach. Unless he had the story all wrong, but the alternate tale was too horrendous to even think about. How could anyone commit such an inhuman act?

But Steve had no choice. With trembling hands, he began rearranging the pieces: the men running, the woman burning, the man holding the baby, the baby in the water, the men gathered around the tree, and finally, the desolate scene.

As he placed the last piece, a chilling story unfolded, making his soul shiver.

A woman was hiding in one of the huts, cradling her baby.

A group of men charged toward the place, shouting, "Come out, Anna! We know you're here. This ends today!"

Their faces were twisted with rage. The baby's cries echoed, drawing them in. Two men barged inside, dragging the woman and her child into the open.

"Please, let me go! I'll disappear and never come back!" she begged, desperation lacing her voice.

"No matter where you go, your bad luck will follow. You have to die, and so does your baby. Your curse is ruining our lives."

"The village has suffered drought and disease ever since you appeared, and that will end today."

They wrenched the baby from her arms and doused her in gasoline, igniting the flames that consumed her screams. The men showed no mercy as they tossed the baby into the water. They gathered at a tree, praying fervently.

"O Lord of the trees! We have rid ourselves of the woman and her cursed child. Grant us peace and happiness once more."

Steve was struck by a wave of horror, rendering him momentarily speechless as the grim scene played out before him. The chilling reality of what he had just witnessed crashed over him like a relentless tide. Before he could fully process the horrors etched into his mind, the square vanished, replaced by the key he had seen earlier—the one adorned with the strange symbol. It floated in the air, beckoning him as if it held the answers he desperately sought. His heart raced, caught between dread and curiosity, but he forced himself to step forward and grasp the key. Just as the cold metal met his palm, the mirrors shifted once more. This time, they revealed the library where they had been staying, the familiar surroundings tinged with an eerie new significance.

"Hey, Steve! The library! Let's go!" Lucas exclaimed, his voice bursting with relief and excitement, but a heavy weight settled in Steve's chest.

"Wait, Lucas. We don't know which one to enter. They all look the same."

"Come on, Steve, lighten up! Not everything needs overthinking. We can go through any of them!"

"If there's one thing I've learned here, it's that nothing is what it seems. So, just wait."

His heart raced as he scanned the mirrors again. Everything appeared identical, yet a gnawing anxiety churned inside him.

Time was running out—only a few grains of sand remained before they would be trapped here forever!

As he scrutinized the reflections, he noticed that most mirrors were merely flipped images of the original library—dusty shelves and dishevelled chairs, distorted but familiar. But one mirror stood apart, reflecting the library with an unsettling clarity, as if it were the true version.

"Lucas!" he shouted, urgency lacing his voice, though he couldn't see his friend. "I think I found it! The right mirror! Run. The correct mirror shows a chair that's slightly tilted to the left. It's the only one that has that! The rest of them have the tilt on the right."

As the last grains of sand slipped through the hourglass, he took a deep breath and moved toward the mirror that showed the library like the original one. Just as he reached it, the mirror transformed into a doorway, the air crackling with anticipation.

CHAPTER NINE

THE MAZE

As Steve entered the library, his heart pounded in his chest, his eyes scanning the dim, shadow-filled room for any sign of Lucas. His anxiety crept in with each passing second. Where was he? Just as Steve began to fear the worst, Lucas appeared from behind a bookshelf. Relief surged through Steve, and he nearly embraced his friend on impulse. They collapsed into chairs, exhausted.

"I think the memories are connected," Steve said, his voice low but urgent. Lucas looked at him, intrigued.

"What do you mean?"

"Remember the man in the first memory, the one who was tied up?"

"Yeah."

"Well, I saw him at the wedding. Someone called him Oliver."

Lucas's eyebrows shot up. "Oliver? That's interesting. But how does that help us find the girl?"

Steve shook his head, frustrated.

"I don't know yet. We've got a locket, a key, and the fact that I'm apparently about to get married—and I didn't even know it," he added with a bitter laugh.

Lucas leaned back, considering. "You think solving the mystery of the missing babies will lead us to her?"

"Maybe. It's the only lead we've got right now." Steve frowned, his mind racing back to the gruesome scene. "But that other memory... how could someone burn a woman alive?"

Silence.

Steve turned to find Lucas fast asleep, the worry on his face replaced by peaceful calm. A small smile tugged at Steve's lips. He closed his eyes, letting exhaustion overtake him.

They both needed the rest for whatever was coming next. Once they were awake and ready, Lucas and Steve decided to search for the soul that would lead them to their next clue. As they stepped outside, an unsettling sight met their eyes: instead of the open land they expected, a massive labyrinth sprawled before them, its walls towering and foreboding. They searched for a way around, but the maze seemed to stretch infinitely in every direction.

"Maybe we need to go through this maze to find the soul," Lucas muttered, his voice barely above a whisper.

They exchanged worried glances, the realization settling in that their only option was to venture into its depths. With a deep breath, they reluctantly stepped inside. The air grew cooler, and the dim light from flickering lamps cast eerie shadows along the walls. Every sound echoed ominously in the stillness. Steve's heart raced, uncertainty gnawing at him.

'What if we can't find our way out?' he thought, his mind racing with the possibilities of what lurked within the maze.

"Stay close," Lucas urged, and they moved cautiously forward, unaware of the trials that awaited them in the darkness ahead.

After walking for some time, Steve realized Lucas was no longer with him. His pulse quickened as he spun in all directions, the maze suddenly feeling more suffocating. He called out Lucas' name, but the sound was swallowed by the twisting paths and dead ends. Every turn felt like another wrong choice, tightening the knot of dread in his chest.

When he finally found Lucas, Steve's relief was quickly replaced by confusion—Lucas was standing perfectly still, his eyes fixed on something ahead, as if carved from stone.

"Lucas?" Steve's voice wavered in the eerie quiet, but there was no response.

As Steve moved closer, he saw what held Lucas in a trance. The hedge in front of them rippled like water, playing out a scene. A group of boys surrounded a smaller figure, their laughter sharp and cruel.

"Look at yourself! You think you can compete with us?" one boy taunted, shoving the smaller boy, who just stood there, trembling and staring at the ground. The boys circled him like predators.

"Just participate in the race and see what happens next," one threatened with a sneer.

The boy looked terrified; his shoulders hunched as if he could disappear into himself. Then, one of them shoved him to the ground.

"Let's make sure this piece of filth doesn't participate at all," another boy spat.

Their sneers turned to malicious smiles as they picked up stones.

The first one struck him with a dull thud, but the others followed, faster and more vicious.

The sharp crack of stone against flesh filled the air, mingling with their cruel laughter. Blood started to bloom on the boy's arms as he shielded his head, silent tears running down his face as the barrage continued. Beside Steve, Lucas's breath turned ragged.

His hands shot up to cover his face, and he mumbled, "Please... please leave me alone. I won't participate... please."

The words were laced with fear, pulling him back into that memory, a boy trapped in a nightmare. Steve's heart sank with the realization—the boy on the ground was Lucas. Acting on instinct, he grabbed Lucas by the shoulders and turned him away from the scene.

"You're not there anymore, Lucas. You're with me. They can't hurt you now," Steve said, his voice steady.

Slowly, Lucas's trembling eased, but the haunted look in his eyes remained, the weight of that memory still heavy in the air. For a long time, they stood in silence, the echo of stones and threats lingering between them.

When they finally walked again, the quiet wasn't peaceful—it was heavy, filled with the spectre of stones, blood, and cruel voices that followed them like shadows.

After a long silence, Lucas finally spoke, his voice subdued, "It happens sometimes. This land shows me memories I really want to forget, but I still can't figure out what triggers it."

Steve glanced at him; concern etched on his face.

"That's alright," he said gently. "What matters is that you're here now, with me."

As they walked, the atmosphere between them began to ease, but just as they were speaking, they arrived at a door that hadn't been there before, with a guard standing tall and imposing in front of it. Both Steve and Lucas hesitated, unsure of how the door had appeared in the middle of the maze. They exchanged a glance but moved cautiously toward it. Before they could get closer, the guard raised a hand, stopping them in their tracks.

"If you want to go ahead," he said in a low, commanding voice, "you must answer my question."

Steve and Lucas exchanged another look, confusion and curiosity flickering in their eyes.

"A question?" Steve asked, his voice edged with uncertainty. "What kind of question?"

The guard's eyes narrowed slightly. "It is to test whether you are worthy of entering."

His voice rumbled like distant thunder, heavy with authority. They didn't know what lay beyond the door, but assuming it might lead them to the soul they were searching for, they nodded in agreement. The guard wasted no time, his tone grave as he asked,

"I am always ahead but never arrive, I make you worry, laugh, or strive. In the unknown, I always reside, What am I that you can't hide?"

Steve and Lucas stood frozen for a moment, the riddle hanging in the air between them like a weight. The words echoed in their minds; the answer elusive yet teasingly close.

They racked their heads for the answer.

"Can the answer be ghost?" Lucas whispered to Steve, his eyes glinting with excitement.

Steve shook his head, feeling a mix of frustration and determination.

"Think, Lucas. What's something that's always ahead of us but never arrives?"

"An animal that we're trying to hunt," Lucas suggested, a wide smile spreading across his face as if he'd struck gold.

Steve raised an eyebrow, sceptical.

"Or it could be an elephant. It's difficult to hide," he replied, shrugging as if that were a perfectly valid answer.

"Honestly, I don't know what I would have done without you, Lucas," Steve said, trying to mask his irritation.

He felt the weight of the riddle pressing down on him, the urgency to solve it clawing at his thoughts. His mind raced as he searched for the right answer, but the more he tried to think, the more tangled his thoughts became.

He momentarily considered 'anticipation,' but quickly dismissed it— it didn't seem right. 'Is it a mirage?' he mused aloud, but that didn't fit either. What's something that makes you worry, laugh, or strive? Frustration bubbled beneath the surface, and he could feel the pressure mounting with every second that ticked by. Just then, Lucas's voice broke through the haze of his mind.

"You think we'll ever be able to solve this riddle?"

"We need to see what the future holds, Lucas," Steve murmured, his heart pounding.

The realization hit him like a flash of lightning illuminating a dark sky. Something that's always ahead yet never arrives, that makes you laugh, worry, and strive, residing in the unknown. With a newfound clarity, he turned to the guard, adrenaline coursing through him.

"The answer is: future."

"Correct. You may go inside," the guard replied, stepping aside with a nod that felt both reassuring and foreboding.

His stern gaze seemed to hint at the challenges lurking beyond the threshold, leaving Steve with an unsettling sense of anticipation.

As they stepped through the door, they found themselves in a vast room lined with shelves of books on all sides. An odd illumination bathed the space, casting soft shadows without any visible source of light.

They scanned the room, their eyes darting around. No other door led them forward, and no soul was present to exchange memories—just endless shelves filled with books that seemed to whisper secrets.

They turned to look back, only to find the door behind them firmly closed. A strange sense of suffocation washed over them, the air thickening in the large room that sprawled before their eyes.

Cautiously, they moved forward, anticipation prickling at their skin as if someone might jump out at them from the shadows.

In a moment of desperation, they began sliding the shelves, hoping to uncover a hidden door, but nothing revealed itself. Turning to the books, they discovered, to their dismay, that all of them were blank. They flipped through several, their hopes rising with each turn of the page, only to be met with a stark emptiness.

Lucas furrowed his brow, holding up a book.

"What's the use of a library if the pages are blank? It's like a joke without a punchline."

Steve glanced at him, a faint smile tugging at the corners of his lips despite the tension.

"Maybe it's a story we don't want to be part of," he replied, frustration colouring his voice.

Steve's hands tightened around the book in his hand, knuckles pale.

"How are we supposed to get out of here?" he muttered, the words escaping his lips as a sigh of despair.

As if in response to his question, words began to appear on the page before him. One by one, letters began to take shape, faintly glowing as if an unseen hand was tracing them into existence. Steve blinked, almost too stunned to speak, as a sentence slowly emerged before his eyes. Lucas peered over his shoulder, eyes narrowing as the words unfolded. A cold shiver ran down his spine. When the final letter appeared, they both stared in silence, reading the message that had materialized from nowhere. It said:

"In darkness, the truth can be found,

Among the pages where dreams abound.

Trace the spines where the stories intertwine,

The letters will guide you, revealing a sign.

Where the tales of old and new unite,

Turn to that shelf to reveal the light."

They looked at each other, eyes wide with amazement. "What does this mean?" Lucas asked, holding up the book as if expecting an answer to leap out.

Steve glanced back at the riddle; his forehead creased in concentration.

"I think it's a clue—a riddle we need to decode to find the exit."

Lucas groaned, running a hand through his hair.

"Another riddle? Seriously?"

Steve blocked out Lucas' frustration, his gaze fixed on the words. He read the clue once again, slowly, each syllable heavy with meaning.

"The first two lines... I think it's saying the answer is hidden in the darkness of these books."

Lucas leaned closer, his voice dropping to a whisper, as though someone might be listening.

"Then the titles—maybe they'll give us a sign."

Steve gave him a quick, impressed nod.

"Good thinking, Lucas. But what about the last two lines?"

Lucas hesitated for a moment, then spoke.

"Maybe... the shelf with the clues is the one where the old and new tales come together?"

Steve raised an eyebrow, the corners of his lips lifting despite the pressure hanging over them.

"You're full of surprises today," he said, but his tone was sharper than before.

"Now, how about telling us what exactly 'old and new tales' means?"

Lucas shrugged, a satisfied grin on his face.

"You can't expect me to do all the hard work, you know."

Steve gave a quick smile, but his focus was already back on the riddle. He read it over again, his brows knit together, trying to make sense of the cryptic lines.

"Old tales... maybe classic literature," he murmured, more to himself than to Lucas.

"New tales... contemporary works. What if it means a shelf where they're placed together? That's where the clue is."

Lucas' eyes lit up.

"That's it, Steve! You're a genius!"

His excitement bubbled over, almost loud enough to echo. They began scanning the shelves, looking for anything that might fit the description.

But as they moved down the rows, their excitement turned to frustration.

The spines of the books were as blank as the pages inside. Steve frowned, running his fingers along the empty spines.

"There's nothing..." Lucas groaned, annoyance edging into his words. "It's like we're chasing shadows. How are we supposed to find anything if the books don't even have titles?"

They even tried speaking to the books, hoping the covers might respond, might reveal something hidden. But nothing changed. The room seemed to mock their efforts, the blank pages offering no answers.

Lucas threw the book in his hand in frustration. As it hit the ground, the surroundings began to change, as if the book had activated a hidden mechanism. The shelves on the right side of the room slid away, revealing an intricate spiral of books intertwined in a mesmerizing pattern, their spines shimmering with an ethereal glow.

Each shelf seemed to pulse softly, as if alive, inviting them into a realm of forgotten stories. Steve and Lucas stared in awe, their mouths agape.

Suddenly, a thought struck Steve like a bolt of lightning: the riddle, 'trace the spines where the stories intertwine,' must refer to these newly revealed shelves. Heart racing, Steve dashed toward the spiral, Lucas close behind.

"Can you believe this? We might actually find something!" Lucas exclaimed; his eyes wide with excitement.

"Let's hope it's something useful," Steve replied, a hint of nervousness in his voice.

He grabbed the nearest book, tracing its spine with trembling fingers. To his relief, the title emerged: *GREAT PERSONALITIES*. He quickly pulled out another book, tracing its spine, which revealed *THEORY OF GRAVITY*. A mix of excitement and dread washed over him as he surveyed the hundreds of books spiralling around them, their spines gleaming under an unseen light. The familiar feeling of helplessness crept back into his chest.

"How are we supposed to find the right books in this vast sea of stories?" he asked, frustration lacing his tone.

Steve took a deep breath, forcing himself to focus. He knew that letting emotions take over wouldn't help them escape this puzzle. Just as he was deciding what to do, Lucas pointed to a particular section of the shelves that glowed softly, casting a warm, golden light across the room.

"Look over there!" Lucas exclaimed, his eyes sparkling with hope.

They approached the glowing shelves and each pulled out a book, tracing their spines, but disappointment washed over them as they revealed titles unrelated to classic or contemporary works. Instead, they were filled with texts about the evolution of the human species and the human developmental processes. Steve opened one of the books, only to find the pages blank, an unsettling reminder of their predicament. He knew that some unknown action would reveal its secrets, but time was slipping away. The riddle had clearly stated that the letters on the spine would provide a clue, and that was what he needed to focus on.

"There's nothing that can help us here," Lucas muttered, his voice barely above a whisper, the weight of despair evident in his tone.

His shoulders slumped, and he cast his gaze downward, as if the shelves themselves were closing in on him.

"Maybe there is!" Steve replied, a spark of hope igniting within him.

He took a deep breath, steadying himself as he recalled the concept of old and new tales uniting.

"We assumed 'old' and 'new' referred to classic and contemporary works, but what if it symbolizes human growth? Old could represent the earliest humans in evolution, while new signifies newborn babies or the latest species in our developmental journey."

Together, they began to examine the glowing section more closely, pulling out books and tracing their spines. Titles like *'HUMAN EVOLUTION'* and *'FROM BIRTH TO DEATH'* met their eyes, reinforcing Steve's theory.

"Wait," Lucas said, holding up two books.

"I just found '*BEYOND THE VEIL*' and '*THROUGH THE LOOKING GLASS.*'

Why are these titles about gates and mirrors among all these texts on evolution? They feel out of place."

"Yeah, I found one too," Steve chimed in, excitement creeping into his voice. "It reads '*THE FORGOTTEN GATE.*'"

Steve frowned, pondering the oddity.

"Maybe they're not out of place at all. Perhaps they're here to guide us to the next step. The riddle mentioned 'the letters on the spine will give us a clue.' What if these titles are part of that clue?"

"Right! If we combine them, they could reveal something important," Lucas agreed, a glimmer of understanding sparking in his eyes.

Steve's expression brightened. *"The Forgotten Gate... Through the Looking Glass... Beyond the Veil...* Together, they might be hinting at a passage or a way to look deeper into this mystery."

He leaned closer to the shelves, a sense of urgency in his voice. "It's like they're guiding us to look beyond the obvious—what if we need to find an actual gate or passage beyond these shelves?"

"It talks about a glass, but we haven't seen one anywhere here, have we?" Steve asked, perplexed, his mind racing to piece together the riddle.

At that moment, Lucas bolted out of the room, surprising Steve with a burst of energy.

"Wait, where are you going?" Steve called, hurrying after him.

Lucas sprinted across the brightly lit space, dodging between shelves and disappearing around a corner that had gone unnoticed until now. Steve followed, his heart pounding. When he caught up, Lucas was standing in front of an imposing, transparent panel.

"Look! I found this earlier when we were searching for the books," Lucas said, pointing to a large sheet of glass covering empty shelves.

Both of them stared at the glass, but no door was visible behind it. The surface was smooth and reflective, showing only the outlines of the room behind them.

"Through the looking glass, it had said," Steve murmured, "and this is the only glass we've seen in here. But where's the forgotten gate?"

Cautiously, Steve reached out and touched the glass.

At his touch, a faint shimmer rippled across the surface, and slowly, an image began to form—a gate, delicate and intricate, etching itself into the glass like a ghostly apparition. Steve and Lucas exchanged startled glances, stepping back as the image solidified.

"I can't believe it," Steve breathed, eyes wide.

He pressed against the glass, but his hand slid right off. The gate was there, but unreachable. They turned around, hoping to see the gate reflected somewhere else in the room, but nothing was behind them.

"It said, 'beyond the veil,'" Lucas said, his voice low and thoughtful.

"We need to find a way to move beyond this glass. But... how?"

Steve stared at the glowing gate, baffled.

"We can see it, but it's like... it's trapped in there. What's keeping us from reaching it?"

Steve and Lucas stood still, staring at the shimmering image of the gate in the glass.

It was right in front of them, clear as day, yet impossible to reach.

No matter how many times they tried to touch it, the glass remained solid, and the gate remained just an illusion.

Lucas ran his fingers through his hair in frustration.

"It's right there! Why can't we just walk through?"

Steve shook his head, racking his brain for any missed detail. "We're missing something," he muttered under his breath. His gaze drifted over the glass and back to the words of the riddle that had been running through his mind. *Through the looking glass... beyond the veil... In darkness, the truth will be found.*

"In darkness..." Steve murmured, his heart beginning to race as the pieces started to click together. "That's it."

Lucas raised an eyebrow, confused.

"What's it?"

"The clue," Steve said, excitement creeping into his voice. "In darkness, the truth will be found. We've been trying to see the gate—trying to look through the glass. But we're not supposed to see it."

Lucas frowned, still not getting it. "What do you mean?"

Steve turned to him, eyes widening. "We have to embrace the darkness. We have to stop *looking*. Maybe the only way to access the gate is if we close our eyes—stop relying on sight and trust that the truth is already there."

Lucas blinked, taken aback. "You think we need to... close our eyes?"

"Yes." Steve nodded firmly. "We've been focusing too much on what we see. The riddle's telling us that in the absence of light—when we can't see—we'll find the way out. The truth is in the darkness."

Lucas stared at him for a moment, then gave a slow nod, the logic starting to sink in.

"Alright. It's worth a shot."

Both of them took a deep breath, standing side by side in front of the glass. They hesitated for a moment, glancing at each other one last time, before shutting their eyes and reaching out toward the glass. With their eyes closed, something shifted. The air around them felt different, thicker, almost alive. As their hands touched the glass, they no longer felt the cold, hard surface they'd been met with before. Instead, their fingers passed through something soft, like fog. A shiver ran down Steve's spine.

"Do you feel that?" Steve whispered.

Lucas nodded silently. They both took a cautious step forward, and instead of being blocked, they moved through the glass as if it were nothing more than air. The cool, damp sensation brushed against their skin as they stepped through the veil, their hearts pounding in their chests. As they moved forward, they heard laughter.

CHAPTER TEN

THE FULL MOON NIGHT

When they were sure they had escaped the confines of the room, they slowly opened their eyes. A dimly lit stage loomed before them, with chairs arranged in a semi-circle. The soul, now in his human form, sat with three other souls, their laughter ringing through the air like mocking chimes.

"So, you made it here, finally. My friends thought I was giving away the memories too easily. They wanted to test your worthiness. I hope you enjoyed the test," he said, a sly grin stretching across his face, as the others joined in their laughter.

Frustration twisted within Steve like a coiled snake, yet he fought to maintain his composure.

"We just need our next clue," he replied, his voice steady, though a storm raged inside him.

"Sure, give me the next memory," the soul responded, his tone dripping with condescension.

Steve took a breath, the weight of the moment settling heavily on his shoulders. He resolved to part with the memory of the day Charlie had been injured—his brother had rushed in to save him, only to be caught in the chaos.

The image of Charlie lying in a hospital bed, pain etched across his face, had haunted Steve. Guilt had burdened him like an insatiable predator; each time he had looked at his brother's bandaged form, he had felt like he had failed him. Charlie had tried to protect him, and now he bore the scars of that sacrifice.

As he prepared to exchange the memory, the pain of that moment was ripped from him, and Steve gasped, as though a wound had been suddenly healed.

Yet, the scar it left was cold, numb, as if he were forgetting part of himself.

With a heavy heart, he surrendered the memory that had haunted him for so long.

Once the exchange was complete, Steve and his companion walked toward the only door in sight, a heavy wooden barrier that led them back to the library.

Each step felt laden with the weight of his sacrifice, as if the very air around him shifted in response to his loss. The familiar surroundings of the library awaited them, but Steve could feel that the experience had altered something within him.

As they stepped into the next memory, something about the land felt oddly familiar. The village surrounding them was the same one they had seen earlier, but this time, the sun was sinking below the horizon, casting long shadows across the empty streets. The hustle and bustle of the wedding was gone, replaced by an eerie silence. Not a single soul stirred. They walked cautiously down the deserted road when, suddenly, a face appeared at the window of a nearby building.

A figure, shrouded in shadows, motioned for them to come inside. Steve and Lucas exchanged a hesitant glance but ultimately stepped through the wooden door. Inside, the house was small but charming, its stone walls adorned with vibrant flowers and hand-painted murals.

The room was bathed in the warm glow of a few lamps, casting soft light on a group of men gathered around a bed.

One of them looked up, eyes narrowing slightly as he spotted Steve.

"Good that you came so soon. And I see you've brought a friend," the man said, his gaze lingering on Steve before shifting to Lucas.

Another man nodded in agreement. "We could use as many helping hands as possible, Ethan."

Steve felt a growing sense of unease. Helping hands? He had no idea what they were talking about, and it was clear that neither did Lucas.

Sensing the tension, Lucas stepped forward, offering a casual smile. "Jeff here didn't tell me much about the task at hand. Does anyone care to offer some details?"

The second man, who had been quietly observing, spoke up. "Logan, tell the guy what's going on," he said, motioning to a third man who sat cross-legged on the bed.

"Sure, Liam," Logan replied, sitting up straighter. His voice took on a serious tone as he began to explain.

"As you might have heard, babies have been going missing from the village on every full moon. Tonight is one of those nights, and we've decided it's time to track down the source behind these disappearances."

Liam spread out a map on the small wooden table in the centre of the room, motioning for everyone to gather around. His lean frame bent over the table, the dim light catching hints of sun-bleached hair and the faint lines of weathered skin that spoke of years spent outdoors. The map was crudely drawn but detailed enough to outline the village and its surrounding areas. With steady hands, he traced a path along the winding river, his focused gaze revealing the calm intensity that made people instinctively follow his lead.

"There are seven of us," Liam began, his voice steady and commanding. "Jack and Charles, you'll guard the north entrance to the village. Logan and Ethan, you take the forest that borders the south side. Steve and his friend," he said, glancing at Lucas, "you'll guard the house where the last baby in the village lives. I'll patrol the roads."

Steve tensed at the thought. The last baby? The weight of their task became even clearer now. Liam continued, his finger tracing the paths on the map.

"It's a small town. No one from the village will be outside tonight, just like we instructed. So, if anyone is out there, they're not supposed to be. If they make a move to take the baby, we'll spot them easily."

He paused, giving everyone a hard look, making sure the gravity of the situation had sunk in.

"Remember the call sign," he added.

Lucas shot Steve a confused glance, his brow furrowing slightly.

"Call sign?" he asked.

Without hesitation, Liam pursed his lips and blew a sharp, distinct whistle, the sound slicing through the air.

"That's the call sign," he said, lowering his voice.

"If anyone sees anything suspicious, blow it loud and clear."

The group exchanged determined looks. Lucas, still appearing unsure but trying to mask it, nodded. Liam folded the map and tucked it away.

"We'll start in half an hour. Be ready."

The air was thick with tension and anticipation, as if the night itself held its breath, waiting. No one spoke, but the unnerving silence was enough to explain the gravity of the task at hand.

Half an hour later, everyone took their respective positions and waited anxiously for any unusual movement. Minutes ticked by but they didn't hear anything beyond their own ragged breaths. The house where Lucas and Steve stood guard was completely still. The baby slept peacefully, unaware of the looming danger, while the mother sat in a corner, horror-stricken, as if waiting for the unknown to strike at any moment. Steve's eyes scanned the surrounding area when something caught his attention.

There, on the wall of the house they were guarding, was a strange symbol etched deep into the stone. He squinted, moving closer. His heart sank—he recognized it.

It was the same symbol from John's hand, and the one carved into the head of the key. The sight of it rooted him to the spot, a chill crawling down his spine.

The symbol seemed to follow them, creeping into every corner of their journey like an ominous shadow.

"Lucas," Steve called quietly, his voice laced with unease.

Lucas joined him, frowning at the symbol.

"Damn. That's... disturbing."

Before they could make sense of it, a noise from inside the house broke the silence. They rushed in, tense, only to find the baby still fast asleep, undisturbed by the commotion. The mother stood by the hearth, trembling, the kettle overturned at her feet.

"I... I accidentally dropped the kettle," she said, her voice thick with anxiety. "Nothing else... yet."

Her eyes darted nervously toward the window.

Steve exchanged a glance with Lucas. The air in the room felt too thick, too still. The symbol outside weighed on them both, like a warning neither could ignore. Whatever was out there, lurking in the shadows, was closing in.

And this time, it felt closer than ever.

Just then, they heard the sign call from the south where Logan and Ethan are guarding.

Something must have come up, but they couldn't leave the baby and the mother unguarded. Steve made a split-second decision, leaving Lucas behind to keep watch. His heart raced as he sprinted toward the sound, adrenaline surging through him. When he arrived, he immediately sensed that something was off. Ethan and Logan exchanged bewildered glances, their faces pale. Other members of the group came rushing in, concern etched on their features.

"What happened? Why did you give the call?" Liam demanded, his voice firm and commanding.

"We didn't!" both Ethan and Logan exclaimed in unison.

"We heard the call too; it came from the trees. But when we went to investigate, there was no one there."

Liam scanned the group, trying to piece together the unsettling situation. His gaze landed on Steve, and he asked, "Where's your friend?"

"I left Lucas to guard the house while I came here to check."

The gravity of the situation crashed over them like a wave.

"The baby!" Charles shouted, panic rising in his voice.

Without another word, the group sprang into action, racing back toward the house. Each hurried step echoed with dread, the weight of their realization pressing down on them. When they burst through the door, their worst fears were realized. The crib was empty. Lucas stood frozen beside it, his face pale with disbelief. The mother cowered in the corner, her hands clasped to her mouth, tears streaming down her face. Steve swallowed the panic rising in his chest and stepped closer to the crib. There, lying where the baby should have been, was a folded piece of paper. With shaking hands, Steve picked it up and unfolded it.

'Tell Lexi to stay away from this or she'll lose her life like her brother.'

Who was Lexi? Was he Michael's sister? Does that mean she's Jefferey's fiancé? As his mind mulled over these thoughts, others gathered around to read it. Before Steve could fully process the first line, his eyes caught on another line, written in smaller, messier handwriting beneath the first:

'Liam, You want to stop us? You don't even know the full extent of what you're chasing. Keep your noses out of it, or you'll end up dead.'

And at the bottom, there was that same symbol again. The one etched on the walls, the one that had been haunting him since the start of this nightmare. It almost seemed to mock him, as if to say: You're not ready for what's coming.

"What happened here?" Jack asked, frustration lacing his voice. "You were here; how did the baby disappear?"

Lucas looked crestfallen, his face a mask of shame, as if he wished he could melt away.

Steve placed a reassuring hand on his shoulder and asked gently, "What happened, Lucas?"

"I was waiting outside the door, keeping an eye on the house. Suddenly, I heard screams from inside. When I opened the door, it was dark, and I could hear footsteps, but before I could figure out what was happening, she lit the lamps again, and the crib was empty. I searched everywhere, but didn't find anything."

Lucas hung his head, his gaze fixed on the ground.

"Now they're even threatening Lexi, as if taking Michael's life wasn't enough," Ethan fumed, his fists clenched in anger.

"And they knew we were waiting for them and about our call sign too," Logan added sceptically, his brows furrowed in concern.

A tense silence fell over the group as they exchanged uneasy glances, suspicion simmering beneath the surface.

"None of us could have done it, so stop giving each other that look," Liam commanded, his voice cutting through the tension.

On a hunch, Steve turned to Liam. "What does the symbol at the bottom mean?"

"That's the symbol etched on each house's wall before their baby is taken away," Liam explained, his expression grave. "We don't know what it signifies, just that it's a sinister one."

Ethan was with the mother, trying to console her.

"We should go and warn Lexi before it's too late," exclaimed Logan, his voice tight with anxiety.

Steve looked at the hour glass, just a quarter of the sand was remaining. Heart pounding with concern for Lexi, the group hurried towards her house.

As they approached, the air grew heavy with an unsettling silence, almost as if even the darkness paused in anticipation.

The front door creaked open, revealing a dark interior that felt unnaturally still, as if it were waiting for something ominous to unfold.

"Lexi!" Jack called, his voice trembling, but the house offered no answer, only a foreboding hush that sent shivers down their spines. They fanned out, searching for any signs of her presence. In her bedroom, Lucas and Steve rifled through the drawers, their hands shaking with a mix of urgency and dread. Suddenly, Steve's fingers brushed against something cool and leather-bound. "Here!" he said, lifting the journal triumphantly.

But just as he opened it to read the first entry, a swirling vortex of light enveloped them, and in an instant, they were pulled back to the library, leaving the eerie silence of the empty room behind. As the world around them shifted, Steve felt a disorienting rush, the familiar surroundings of the library materializing around them. The sudden transition left him momentarily breathless, the weight of the empty house still heavy in his chest.

"What just happened?" Lucas asked, glancing around the library as if expecting to see Lexi's name written on the walls.

"We were just—" "Searching for answers," Steve interrupted, gripping the journal tightly, its worn cover now a symbol of the urgency they felt. "We have to find out what's in this."

They quickly settled themselves behind a table and opened the journal, flipping through pages filled with entries of recent months. But it was the last few entries that caught their attention. One read:

'Michael's death has left me alone in this big world, but not without a purpose. He was close to the truth, and he knew it. He feared for his life, and so he shared everything with me.'

"Wow! This girl is in some serious trouble," Lucas muttered under his breath.

With growing anticipation, they continued reading. The next entry was even more chilling. Drawn on the page was the symbol that had been haunting them for so long: a skull with two crossed bones. Notes were scrawled beside it:

'Symbol of a sinister gang that has operated in the west for decades. Meddling with them means inviting death.'

Near the bottom of the page, more words were hastily scribbled:

'I'm not afraid of death, not anymore. I will finish what my brother started.'

Steve and Lucas exchanged worried glances. Lexi wasn't just caught in something dangerous—she was determined to confront it head-on. The next entry was a game changer.

'Jeff thinks I should stay away from this mission. He's scared for my life, but he has to understand that being a witch comes with responsibilities.'

"A wi...witch?" Lucas stammered, his eyes widening. "You mean, real powers and all? I always knew something was off, but this? This is too much."

Steve shook his head, trying to wrap his mind around the revelation.

"We've been chasing shadows and clues. Maybe this is just another mystery we don't fully understand yet."

Before they could process it fully, the final entry made them both tense up, their breath catching in their throats:

'This horror will end sooner than anyone thinks. I'll be heading there...soon. The time has come. It's now or never. I hope Jeff knows how much I love him. He'll never understand, but this is my choice. If I don't come back...'

Steve's fingers tightened around the pages, his pulse quickening. Lucas leaned in closer, voice barely a whisper. "She's planning something, isn't she? Something big." Steve nodded, his eyes scanning the final words. "And she's going to face it alone," he murmured, the burden of the statement settling over them like a suffocating cloud. The remaining pages were blank, as if too afraid to carry the weight of the words that might have come next.

Steve's gaze lingered on the words *"I hope Jeff knows how much I love him."* His chest tightened as a familiar feeling crept in. He understood the weight of those words. The desperation to shield someone you care about, even if they don't understand. Lexi wasn't just chasing answers—she was risking everything to protect the people she loved, just like he would.

"She's doing this for him," Steve murmured, more to himself than to Lucas. "She knows it could cost her everything, but she's willing to face it alone if it means keeping him safe."

He swallowed hard, feeling a heavy pull in his gut. He'd been there before—standing on the edge, willing to throw himself into the fire for the sake of someone else. And now, Lexi was doing the same.

CHAPTER ELEVEN

LEXI

Something was bothering Steve as they set out to complete the next exchange with the soul. The name Jeff kept echoing in his mind, a nagging sense of recognition tugged at him each time he heard it—especially when he read it in Lexi's journal. Why did it feel like it belonged to him? He was still wrestling with these thoughts when they stumbled upon the soul standing right in front of them.

Before the soul could say anything, Steve asked, "In one of the memories, someone tried to trap us in a mirror room, and he said he was working for someone. Did you send him?"

"You might as well save that accusing tone if you want those clues anymore, boy," the soul said aggressively. "To answer your question, you're sharing a piece of yourself with this land when you give away your memories, making you vulnerable. You didn't think this land would be a bed of roses, did you?"

"What does that supposed to mean?" Steve retorted, his fists clenching.

"It means the more memories you give away, the more chances you'll face challenges not meant for you. That's the rule of the land."

Steve didn't know how to argue with that, so he proceeded with the memory exchange. He was parting with the memory of his favourite pet, Lola, who had died when he was twelve.

The puppy had been his best friend; they played all day, ate together, and curled up to sleep side by side.

Lola had succumbed to undiagnosed heart disease, and after her death, he could never bring himself to look at another puppy again.

After the exchange, Lucas watched as Steve's eyes glazed over, the faintest flicker of loss crossing his face.

"Another one gone," Lucas muttered, feeling the air between them grow heavier.

Steve and Lucas wandered back to the library, lost in their thoughts, the familiar scent of old books and warped wood enveloping them. Before they realized it, they stood at the door of the library, the weight of the next clue hanging in the air.

The setting of the next memory was strikingly different from the earlier ones. A busy street buzzed with vehicles and people moving in a blur, the scene almost overwhelming for the eyes. Tall buildings loomed over every inch of land, their storefronts brimming with customers. Steve and Lucas exchanged bemused glances, taking in the vibrant chaos around them. Just then, a girl in her late twenties walked up to them, her presence cutting through the din of the street. She was of medium height, carrying an unassuming charm. Her soft features seemed both familiar and inviting. Shoulder-length chestnut hair framed her face, occasionally falling over her hazel eyes, which sparkled with a hint of mischief. A light dusting of freckles across her nose lent her an air of innocence, making her seem approachable. Dressed in a casual outfit of earthy tones—a simple shirt and well-worn jeans—she radiated a laid-back vibe.

As she approached them, she said, "Jeff, how come you're here? I told you I'd be safe," her voice soft yet laced with concern.

Steve stammered, completely at a loss for who the girl was. Just then, as if the heavens were on his side, a waitress in an apron came running toward her.

"Ma'am, you left your purse back in the restaurant!" she panted, breathless from her sprint.

As she handed it over, a paper slipped out and fluttered to the ground. Steve bent down to retrieve it, and his heart skipped a beat as he saw the name: *Lexi*. As the waitress dashed back, Lexi turned her attention back to him. He knew he had to speak soon, his mind racing.

"I know you're capable of taking care of yourself, Lexi, but I couldn't just leave you here alone."

When Lucas heard the name, he shot Steve a puzzled look. Steve nodded, shoving the bill into Lucas's hands.

"Okay, I suppose there's no use arguing with you. Let's solve this mystery together," Lexi said, eyeing Lucas with scepticism.

"Oh, he's a friend of mine, Lucas. He wanted to come along. Can't argue with him either," Steve replied, a mischievous smile playing at his lips as determination surged within him.

"So, what's the plan?" Steve asked, keeping his tone casual despite the flutter in his chest.

"There's a potential lead in this city that can help us locate the gang behind the baby disappearances. I was just about to go there before I saw you," she replied, her voice soft yet determined.

The fire in her hazel eyes sparked something in him. He couldn't help but lean in slightly, drawn by her presence. Lucas nudged him gently, pulling Steve back to reality.

"Let's go then!" Steve exclaimed, a bit too eagerly, as he tried to mask the warmth creeping into his cheeks.

They took a bus to **456 Oak Street, Willow Crescent, Vancouver**. Steve settled next to Lexi, her energy radiating like sunlight, while Lucas slid into a seat behind them.

As the bus rolled through the bustling streets, Lexi pointed out the window, her excitement infectious. "Look, Jeff! It's the same fair my dad used to take us to when we were kids!"

Her enthusiasm ignited a smile on Steve's face, and he caught himself studying her—the way her eyes lit up with each word, the gentle way she moved her hands. Here was a girl on a dangerous mission, yet her laughter rang out like a melody, casting aside the shadows of danger around them. For a moment, the world outside faded, and all he could see was her spark of innocence amidst the chaos.

When they arrived at their destination, a man in his fifties opened the door. After brief introductions, he ushered them inside and motioned for them to sit. The house looked like it hadn't been cleaned for days. Clothes lay in heaps, and cobwebs gathered in the corners. Once they were seated, the old man offered tea and biscuits. Lexi didn't waste time.

"You mentioned in your letter that you had a lead."

"Ah, yes, the lead," the man said, nodding. "I was at a bar when I overheard some men talking at a nearby table.

They mentioned taking babies to a rundown factory in West Wexshire.

At first, I didn't think much of it, but when I saw their faces... they didn't look like men who'd be carrying babies for fun.

And with the news about missing babies in your village, I knew I had to contact you."

"Thank you, Mr. White. You did the right thing by informing us," Lexi said, gratitude clear in her voice. "You've been a great help."

"Did they mention when they'll be taking the babies there?" Steve asked, his voice tinged with curiosity.

"No, I couldn't hear that much," Mr. White admitted. "The bar was too noisy."

After thanking the man for his hospitality and help, they left, the weight of his information hanging over them.

Steve found himself stealing glances at Lexi more often than he'd like to admit, only to catch Lucas's amused looks in response. After doing some reasearch, they took the bus to reach their destination and then a few wrong turns and dead ends before they finally found the rundown factory in West Wexshire just as the sun began to set. The building loomed large before them, with crumbling bricks and scorched walls, evidence of an old fire. The windows were shattered, and the door hung crookedly on its hinges.

"Perfect place for a crime," Lucas muttered.

Hearts racing, they hurried inside, bracing themselves for whatever horrors might be waiting. But the factory was empty. They scoured every inch, but not a single soul—let alone any sign of babies—was anywhere to be found.

"Maybe Mr. White heard wrong. He did say the bar was noisy," Steve said, frustration creeping into his voice.

"Or he was just spinning tales to amuse himself," Lucas added, equally annoyed.

Lexi, however, remained silent, her eyes fixed on the factory's charred walls as if expecting something to reveal itself.

"Wait here a minute," she said suddenly, dashing out of the factory. Steve made a move to follow her, but before he could, that familiar sensation of being pulled by an unseen force hit him. In a flash, he and Lucas were back in the library.

"Wait, what?" Steve blinked in confusion. "How are we back in the library already? Lexi still needs us, and we didn't find any clue or object yet." His voice brimmed with disbelief.

"Maybe we don't get clues or objects in every memory," Lucas replied casually, as if the answer was obvious. "Sometimes, things are just dead ends, like in real life."

"But did you see the way you were looking at her? Man, Jeff—or whatever your name is—you've got it bad!" Lucas added, smirking.

"I wasn't—wait, no, that's not it..." Steve trailed off, turning away from Lucas.

He was sure his cheeks had flushed, and Lucas had likely noticed. Steve sat in a quiet corner, his thoughts spinning around Lexi. There was something off about how he felt when he was near her. Sure, she was attractive—there was no denying that—but it felt superficial. The connection didn't go any deeper than admiration. It felt... hollow. Like he was observing someone from a distance, not standing beside them. There was no real bond, just the surface-level charm of a stranger.

CHAPTER TWELVE

A RED HERRING

The memory exchange with the soul went smoothly, yet, the sweetness of the memory left him like a melody fading into the distance. He tried to hum the tune, but the notes escaped him, leaving only the sense that something beautiful had once played there. This time, he had given up the memory of his first crush in return for their next clue. It was a Christmas party—he had been too nervous to ask her to dance, but she had shyly approached him. They had danced for three songs, his heart soaring with happiness, followed by shared snacks that made him feel like he was on top of the world. He had held onto that memory for years, but now, in the face of more pressing matters, he had no choice but to let it go. Losing something so cherished was the only way to gain something vital.

This clue was of the same city they were in before but a different street.

They were standing in a library full of people engrossed in the book they held.

The scent of aged paper filled the air, and the soft rustling of pages created a quiet hum. No one seemed to notice their abrupt entry. They looked around for a familiar face. Just then they heard a whisper.

"Jeff, here."

They turned around and were surprised to see Lexi sitting at a table with some newspapers sprawled in front of her. Steve and Lucas hurried over to join her.

"Where were you guys? You left me alone at the factory. I looked for you everywhere.", her annoyance tinged with concern as she stared at them with crossed arms.

Steve thought quickly. "We thought we saw a shadow lurking near one of the windows; so, we went after him but he escaped."

"Oh! Tough luck. And how did you know I'll be here?"

"My friend here is pretty good at guess game.", Lucas chimed in.

Steve quickly shifted the topic. "So, what did you find in those papers?"

Lexi leaned closer, her voice dropping to a hushed tone. "I've been tracing incidents around the state. They all involve missing babies. It's not just our village—babies have been disappearing from other places too. And the police haven't been able to trace the kidnappers at all. It's as if they just vanish into thin air."

"That sounds chilling.", added Lucas.

"Yes, and I have reasons to believe that people behind these crimes are in this city itself."

"I hope your reasons are better than Mr.White's hearing," Lucas said somewhat sarcastically.

Steve shot him a warning look, but Lexi ignored the remark, her focus entirely on the matter at hand.

"Do you think, the rundown factory was a ruse or they cleared out before we could get them?", asked Steve.

"I have been thinking about it. There were no traces of anyone being there. No beds, no leftover food or trash. I think it was a ruse or a genuine mistake by Mr. White."

"So, how do we find this gang?" Steve inquired.

Lexi's eyes narrowed.

"We're going to stake out a hospital. A man fitting the description—white hair, short, crooked walk— is likely to show up there tonight. If we follow him, we might find their hideout."

Lucas leaned in close and whispered to Steve, "Remember the last time I helped with a stakeout? I lost a baby right in front of me. I don't want anything to go wrong this time."

Steve placed a hand on his shoulder, his tone gentle but firm. "It wasn't your fault, Lucas. You did everything you could. Stop blaming yourself."

Reluctantly, Lucas nodded, and they agreed to proceed. They found themselves sitting in a rented van, parked just across from the hospital's main entrance.

Tension hung thick in the air as they watched the door, each afraid of missing a vital clue. Minutes blurred into hours, and still no sign of the man they were after. Lucas was starting to doze off when Lexi suddenly leaned over, her voice soft but affectionate.

"I'm glad you're here, Jeff," she said, her eyes lingering on him. Steve felt a rush of adrenaline as she took his hand.

"I'm just glad you're not alone in this," he replied, though he wasn't sure if his heart was racing from the thrill of the mission or the warmth of her touch.

Just then, his gaze snapped to the entrance.

"Wait—look!" He pointed to a man hobbling toward the hospital doors, fitting the description exactly. Lucas woke up with a jerk. The three of them froze, pulses quickening.

"I'll go inside, see what he's up to, and then we can follow him when he leaves the hospital," Lucas offered, a bit too eagerly, as if trying to make up for his past mistake.

Steve hesitated but knew this might ease some of Lucas's guilt. "Alright, be careful," he said, nodding.

Minutes passed. Neither Lucas nor the man they were tailing had returned. Steve shifted in his seat, his worry growing.

He was just about to head inside to check when a sleek black sedan pulled up to the hospital entrance.

A group of masked men with guns swiftly emerged from the vehicle. Steve's stomach dropped as they stealthily made their way inside. Suddenly, chaos erupted.

The muffled sound of gunshots followed by frantic screams cut through the air.

Steve's first instinct was to bolt out of the van and save Lucas, but Lexi grabbed his arm, her voice trembling.

"No, Jeff. Don't! It's too dangerous."

"Lucas is in there! I have to help him," Steve shot back, his voice rising in panic.

"You can't," she pleaded, gripping his arm tighter. "They have guns. You'll only end up as another hostage. We need to call the police."

"There's no time, Lexi! You heard those shots. Lucas could be hurt!"

Steve's heart pounded as the sense of urgency overtook him. Without waiting for her reply, he wrenched his arm free, threw open the van door, and sprinted toward the hospital.

He slipped through the back door and into the hospital's dispensary, immediately greeted by chaos. The lights flickered overhead, casting eerie shadows as terrified patients huddled behind overturned chairs and medical trolleys.

The goons from earlier were prowling the halls, their footsteps heavy, searching for their next target.

Nurses crouched low, whispering frantic reassurances to anyone nearby, but panic was thick in the air. Steve's heart raced as he scanned the room. Then, behind a toppled table, he spotted Lucas, his face pale, clutching his leg in agony.

"Steve, my leg—" Lucas winced, his face pale as he tried to move.

Steve crouched beside him. "Don't worry, we'll get you out of here."

But before Steve could plan their escape, Lexi appeared from the shadows. Her face was tense, eyes darting around the hospital like a trapped animal.

"Jeff, we have to go! Now!" she urged; her voice almost frantic.

"What about Lucas? He's hurt. We can't just leave him here," Steve said, his tone incredulous.

Lexi hesitated, then leaned closer, whispering urgently in his ear, "We'll be caught if we stay. They'll kill us. We have to save ourselves."

Steve stared at her, stunned. This wasn't the Lexi he knew—the girl who was ready to give everything for her village, for others.

"We're not leaving him," Steve said, shaking off her suggestion.

He hoisted Lucas onto his back, and together they moved slowly toward the exit, the sound of gunfire and frantic shouts still echoing behind them. Once they were safely inside their van, Lexi turned to Steve and said, "Jeff, I'm sorry. I didn't mean to leave your friend behind. I was just afraid that I'll lose the one person I have in this world." Steve nodded, though the unease bothered him. He turned his attention to Lucas, focusing on tending to his friend's wound.

"We have to find a way to save those people," Steve said, urgency sharpening his tone. "We need to round up the gang and end this nightmare once and for all."

"No, Jeff. We don't even know if these attackers are from that gang," Lexi argued, her voice tight. "Even if they are, catching them now will just tip off their leader. He'll escape, and we'll lose our chance."

"But in your journal, you were determined to face the danger head-on," Lucas retorted, a challenge in his voice.

Lexi stiffened, looking somewhat offended. "Yes, because my goal is to take down their leader—not just these foot soldiers. That's how we end this for good."

Before Steve could reply, the distant wail of police sirens filled the air. Help was coming, but something still felt off to Steve.

They were exhausted, so they decided to drop Lexi at the motel she was staying. While driving, Steve suddenly remembered something. "Oh, and when I was inside, I had seen a symbol of a roaring lion stitched on their sleeves. Do you know anything about that?", he asked Lexi.

She barely hesitated before replying. "It's the symbol of the gang we're after. It means they see themselves as kings around here, ruling over everything.", her voice calm but a little too quick.

Steve frowned. He distinctly remembered reading in her journal that their symbol was of a skull and crossed bones, the one that appeared over and over again in their journey. When he brought it up, she shifted uncomfortably.

"That... must have been an old symbol they used. Gangs change their marks sometimes, you know, to throw people off," she said, her explanation rushed but smooth enough to let the moment pass. Steve nodded, not entirely convinced, but let the matter drop—for now.

They reached the motel and exchanged goodbyes. Just as Steve was about to start the engine and head to return the rented van, a familiar disorienting pull gripped him. The world around them shimmered, and before Steve could even take it in, he and Lucas were back in the library—this time bathed in sunlight and a gentle breeze.

Steve realized that ever since meeting Lexi, the once-dark library had transformed into a brighter, more cheerful place, mirroring his own shifting emotions.

Sunshine poured in, the cool air flowed, and faint birdsong filled the room, though no birds were ever in sight.

Steve blinked, disoriented. "Not again," he muttered. Lucas, still nursing his injured leg, groaned in frustration. "You'd think by now we'd get a warning before being yanked back here."

"Don't you think it's odd that in the first few memories, we raced against time to complete a task, and now, for the past two clues, we're just yanked back without learning anything?" Steve asked while examining Lucas' wound, frustration edging into his voice.

Lucas winced as Steve tightened the bandage but kept his tone calm. "We did learn something this time."

"What? That the gang changed their symbol?"

Lucas gave a small nod. "Yeah, it's an important piece of information. Otherwise, we'd be chasing the wrong people. It's like the game's changing. We just don't know why."

Steve leaned back, the weight of Lucas' words pressing down on him. He recalled the earlier memories—the ticking clock, the constant pressure to solve each piece before it was too late. It had always felt like they were racing against time, every second filled with urgency. But now...now they were just yanked back, as if someone else was deciding when the game was over. The inconsistency troubled at him, but he couldn't pinpoint why.

"Yeah, maybe you're right," he muttered, but the unease didn't leave him. Instead, it deepened. He stared at Lucas for a moment before admitting, "There's something else that's been bothering me."

"Tell me, mate."

Steve hesitated, then sighed. "I'm feeling guilty about being attracted to Lexi."

Lucas raised an eyebrow. "Why's that bothering you?"

Steve looked down; his voice quiet. "Think about it, Lucas. She's Jeffery's fiancée, not mine. I know she doesn't realize it, but I do. Yet, when I'm around her, my heart flutters. And I'm letting her get close to me. I'm losing focus."

Lucas leaned back, considering his response. "Look, Steve, this is just a memory. You didn't choose to be here, and it's not like you're stealing her from Jeffery. These feelings—they're not wrong. Just don't let it cloud your judgment."

Steve nodded, though Lucas' words didn't fully ease the guilt tightening his chest. "I guess you're right. I just...need to keep my head straight."

"You will," Lucas said, giving him a reassuring pat on the shoulder. "Remember what really matters: we're here to find answers. The real world's waiting for us out there."

Steve nodded again, though his thoughts were far from settled.

The feelings for Lexi weren't just a distraction—they were a complication. And in a place where nothing seemed to make sense anymore, complications could be dangerous.

"By the way, I never properly thanked you for saving my life back there!" Lucas said, a grin breaking through the pain.

Steve smiled and clapped him on the shoulder. "That's what friends are for!" he exclaimed, his tone light, though the weight of their journey still lingered in his mind.

CHAPTER THIRTEEN

SCAVENGER HUNT

The next memory Steve relinquished was of a picnic his family had with their neighbours at a nearby beach. He could almost taste the salt in the air and feel the warmth of the sun on his skin as he remembered building castles in the sand and sharing his favourite foods with friends. Those carefree days symbolized a simpler time, and parting with this memory felt like letting go of the child within him. But he understood the necessity of this sacrifice.

Unlike their usual explorations in open spaces, this time, they found the soul within a mysterious building. Inside, a circular hall spun endlessly, disorienting them with its dizzying motion. Surrounding the hall were numerous doors, each one a potential pathway to another memory. With careful deliberation, they opened each door, only to discover empty rooms that felt oddly significant, as if they were waiting for the right cues to come alive. To avoid retracing their steps, they marked each door they explored.

At last, in the final room they opened, they found the soul sitting on the ground, lost in a trance. When he noticed them, a faint smile crossed his lips. "Ah! So, you found my pleasure place," he said, looking around at the empty space as if it held some secret joy. Steve and Lucas exchanged glances, puzzled by what could be pleasurable about an empty room, but they pressed forward to complete the memory exchange, the weight of nostalgia heavy in the air.

This new clue led them back to the motel where they had last dropped off Lexi in the previous memory.

They approached her room, knocking lightly before she opened the door, barely glancing up from the paper in her hand. "I was just waiting for you guys," she said, her attention still fixed on the page.

Steve, noticing her distraction, asked, "What's that in your hand?" Lexi held up the paper, her expression unreadable. "I found this letter in front of my door this morning. No idea who left it. No name, no address."

Curious, Steve leaned over her shoulder to read the hurried scrawl:

Flash mob, on road number 18. Clues in the hunt. Planning something big. Want to know more? Reach there by 5 today.

"Woah, that's some message," Lucas chimed in, glancing over as well. His usual nonchalance had an edge of caution this time.

"It's 4:50 now. We can make it if we leave right away," Lexi pointed out, checking the time.

Lucas frowned; tension clear in his voice. "Hold on. This could be a hoax or worse—another trap. Someone could be setting us up."

Lexi folded the letter, meeting his eyes. "Maybe. But we won't know for sure unless we go, right?" Steve couldn't help but admire her courage and determination.

As they headed toward their destination, Steve remarked, "We don't even know if it's related to the gang, we're after. I hope it won't be the hospital scene all over again."

When they arrived at the scene, it was a chaotic spectacle of celebration.

The streets were alive with music, and dancers dressed as lions moved energetically to the thundering beats pouring from the speakers.

Vibrant colours and masks filled the air with excitement, but there was an unsettling edge to the festivities.

"Hey, Steve," Lucas shouted over the noise. "Remember the lion symbol those attackers were wearing? Do you think it's connected to these people dressed as lions?"

Steve narrowed his eyes, scanning the crowd. "I don't know. We'll have to find out," he replied, his voice barely cutting through the blaring music.

Suddenly, the music cut off, leaving an eerie silence hanging over the crowd. A voice boomed through the speakers, catching everyone's attention. "The time has come for the event you've all been waiting for—the scavenger hunt. Find the clues, get the prize. Simple enough. Unless, of course... someone finds more."

The speaker's tone was laced with something ominous, and for a brief moment, Steve felt the man's gaze lock onto them. His eyes flickered with something unreadable. Steve's heart raced, but he quickly shook off the feeling. *Just a coincidence,* he told himself.

The crowd burst into wild applause, unaware of the hidden dangers that might be lurking beneath the surface of this seemingly harmless game.

Everyone crowded around the stage to grab their first clue, as Steve and his friends joined the rush. Their clue came on a small, brightly coloured piece of folded paper. Once they had it, they moved away from the chaotic crowd to a quiet spot where they could talk privately. Opening the paper, they read the message together: *Start your journey where the children play, and follow the path that fades away.* The words hung in the air for a moment as they all studied the simple riddle.

"That sounds pretty straightforward. No hidden clues that I can see here," commented Lucas, shrugging.

Lexi remained silent, her eyes fixed on the words written on the paper, as if she hadn't heard Lucas at all. "Let's find a playground or a park nearby," she said decisively, snapping out of her focus.

They wandered through the streets, turning a few corners until they reached a small park with faded swings and a rusty slide.

Steve glanced at the playground and sighed. "This is where children belong—laughing, playing—not in the hands of strangers, facing the unknown," he muttered, thinking about the missing babies.

Lexi stopped; her expression unreadable as she stared at the swings. "Is it just a coincidence that the first clue mentioned children, or is this the introduction to something bigger?" she asked, her voice low and thoughtful.

"Yeah, now I think you're overthinking this," Lucas replied, folding his arms. He wasn't buying into the paranoia.

Steve looked between them, realizing he was once again caught in the middle of their different approaches. Lucas was practical, while Lexi often chased shadows that sometimes turned out to be more than they seemed.

"No, think about it," Lexi pressed, her voice gaining urgency. "The clue could be meant for someone specific in the crowd, someone who's part of something darker. This whole game might just be a front to pass secret messages."

Steve raised an eyebrow. "But why go through all this trouble? Why not just use simpler methods to deliver a message?"

Lexi didn't miss a beat. "Maybe they're afraid of being watched—maybe this is the safest way to communicate without drawing attention. They're hiding in plain sight."

Her conviction made Steve pause. There was something almost too sure in her voice, and it made him uneasy. Was Lexi jumping to conclusions just because she wanted to see a conspiracy in every corner? Or was she onto something?

He wanted to trust her instincts, but there was a nagging voice in his head telling him she could be seeing patterns that weren't there.

Still, with no other clues at hand and the pressure of time weighing on them, Steve decided to follow her lead.

"Alright," he said, glancing at the park once more. "Let's see where this takes us."

Encouraged by Steve's words, Lexi continued her train of thought. "If the children refer to the missing babies, then the path that fades away could mean the trail going cold in the investigation."

Lucas raised an eyebrow, the look on his face making it clear that he wasn't about to indulge this theory. "Right. Or it's just a game."

Steve didn't want to hurt anyone's feelings, so he offered a gentle compromise. "Okay, Lexi, let's assume that's what this message means," he said, feeling Lucas's gaze boring into him. "At least for now," he added quickly.

"So, where does that leave us?" Steve asked, glancing around the area as if hoping for something to clarify their next step.

"I think the next clue will clear things up for us," Lexi replied, her voice almost eager, like a child presenting evidence to a parent.

Steve hesitated for a moment, scanning the surroundings again. The playground looked normal enough, but beyond it, an overgrown path twisted into the woods, barely visible under layers of fallen leaves. An unused path... could that be it?

"Okay," he said, more to himself than to the others. "I see an unused path there. Lets follow it and see where it leads."

Other people were starting to come towards the park, but Steve, Lexi, and Lucas kept moving, following the overgrown path.

The air grew still as they ventured deeper, the crunch of dried leaves and snapping branches the only sound accompanying them. The path narrowed, twisting through the trees, until they reached a small clearing. In the middle of the clearing, neatly arranged in a circle, were stuffed bears. Dozens of them, sitting upright, their beady eyes staring blankly ahead.

Lexi's face scrunched in confusion. "What is this, a carnival game?"

Lucas moved towards the bears and picked one up, turning it in his hands. "Look—there's a little tag under this one's paw." He unfolded a small piece of paper hidden beneath the bear's paw, and it read: *Follow the river's flow, where the roses grow.*

He raised an eyebrow. "Seems harmless. Probably another clue for the game," he said, glancing at the growing crowd.

Steve picked up another bear, checking it closely. Sure enough, it also had a tag, and the message was simple: *Climb the hill, see the sun until.*

"They all have clues," Steve murmured.

"But... something about this feels too easy."

Lexi wasn't listening. She was scanning the circle, her eyes darting between the bears. She crouched by one near the edge and tilted her head. "Wait a second... look at this one."

Steve and Lucas followed her gaze. The bear she pointed to had a subtle difference. Unlike the others, which were pristine, this one had a slight tear at its side, barely noticeable unless you were looking closely.

"This one's been tampered with," Lexi whispered. She gently picked it up, and when she squeezed it, the stuffing felt lumpy, uneven. "There's something inside."

"Let's open it," Steve said, exchanging a glance with Lucas.

Lucas tore open the stitching, spilling the cotton to the ground. Inside, hidden deep in the stuffing, was a folded piece of paper. They quickly opened it. The handwriting was different from the previous clues—hurried, almost frantic. It read:

Find the flower that grows in the dark, hidden beside the oak with a mark.

Lexi's fingers brushed over the words.

"The flower that grows in the dark... That's no ordinary clue. It's like it's meant for someone who knows more."

Steve nodded. "The other bears had clues for the participants, but this one... this one feels like it's meant for someone in on the real game."

"You still think it's just a game?" Lexi's voice trembled slightly; her frustration evident as she looked pointedly at Lucas.

"We'll see when your clues solve the mystery of the missing babies," Lucas shot back, clearly not buying into her interpretation.

Steve quickly stepped in, sensing the tension rise. "Where do you think we can find a flower that grows in the dark?" His voice was calm, trying to divert the argument, though the question seemed more directed at himself than either of them.

"It could be literal," Lexi said, her eyes narrowing, deep in thought. "But it could also be a metaphor... for something hidden, something dangerous."

Lucas smirked, about to offer a sarcastic reply, but then his expression shifted.

"Moonflower!" he blurted, catching them both off guard.

"It's the only flower that blooms in the dark."

Steve and Lexi exchanged surprised glances. "That's... actually a good point," Lexi admitted, the surprise evident in her voice.

"But where do we find a moonflower around here?" Steve asked, the gears in his mind turning, wondering what unexpected twist might lie ahead.

"If these clues are in fact intended for someone in the crowd, won't they realise we're after them too?", asked Lucas.

"I'm surprised no one jumped on us yet, unless...", he looked at Lexi before completing his sentence. "this is just a game and we should be chasing the real clues that will lead us to the gang.

Lexi's brows furrowed at Lucas's words, but she didn't respond. Steve, on the other hand, couldn't shake the gnawing questions swirling in his mind.

Is this even worth it? His eyes flicked back to the hourglass. The sand was slipping through so quickly, just like the memories he had sacrificed.

What if it's all a distraction? What if we're chasing ghosts while the real answers are somewhere else, out of reach?

Frustration churned inside him. Each time they exchanged a memory, he felt more fragmented, like parts of him were slipping away, never to return. And for what? A trail that kept leading them in circles, while the gang—the ones responsible for the missing babies—stayed one step ahead.

Steve clenched his fists. *Was this another dead end? How much more was he willing to lose just to find out.* "Let's just find the next clue and hope it'll give us some answers," Steve said, trying to mask the growing frustration tightening in his chest. They asked around about the moonflower, but most people seemed oblivious to what it was. Just as they were about to give up, an old man from a nearby antique shop leaned in, intrigued by their inquiry.

"There's an old cemetery," the man said, his voice raspy but certain. "A forgotten garden by the graves... It's the only place you'll find a moonflower in this city. I visit often," he added softly, "my wife rests there."

Steve exchanged a quick glance with Lexi and Lucas, feeling a mix of hope and dread.

They hurried to the cemetery, the weight of the day's events pressing down on them.

As they walked, Steve glanced at Lexi, a thought nagging at him.

"Lexi, if you want to wait outside for this clue, that's alright," he offered gently.

Lexi turned to him with a questioning look, her expression unreadable.

"I mean, we know the weight of your brother's death is still heavy on your chest. So, I'm not sure if the cemetery is the right place for you right now." Concern laced his voice, but Lexi just shrugged.

"Oh, that! I'm fine, Steve. Don't worry about me." Her tone was distant, almost robotic, and it sent a chill through him.

Lucas leaned closer, whispering, "Isn't she a bit too okay for someone who recently lost her brother?"

Steve nodded slowly, eyeing Lexi as she stared ahead, her arms crossed tightly over her chest. "Maybe she doesn't want to get weepy in front of us," he suggested, though a gnawing feeling in his gut told him there was more to it.

The man's directions guided them through narrow, overgrown paths until they reached the garden. It looked abandoned, wild plants choking the headstones.

In the middle of it all stood the moonflower, its pale petals glowing faintly in the twilight.

Next to it, an old oak tree loomed, its gnarled branches spreading like fingers. Steve's breath caught when he saw it—on the trunk was a freshly marked X. The bark around the mark seemed splintered, and a small hole gaped beside it, as though waiting.

Lexi knelt by the tree. "It's like someone left this for us," she whispered. Her hand trembled as she reached into the hole.

Steve's pulse quickened. What if this is where they uncover something more than they bargained for? She pulled out a folded paper.

It read: *Look for the bell that never rings, and the bird that never sings.*

"Let me guess," Lucas said, his voice dripping with sarcasm.

"The bell could mean a revolver, and the bird represents the babies. So, what? They're shooting babies with revolvers? Isn't that right, Lexi?"

Lexi shot him an incredulous look. "You know you could be more helpful if you used your brain instead of your tongue," she snapped back, her frustration bubbling over.

Turning to Steve, she softened her tone slightly. "What do you think this clue means?"

Steve felt caught in the middle again, like a referee in a match he didn't want to officiate. Though lingering doubts about the hunt tugged at him, he weighed his words carefully. "I think we need to find a broken bell and maybe a statue of a bird for our next clue."

"Or it could hint at a silent way of transmitting information, without making noise—like this whole hunt," Lexi added, her determination shining through despite the tension.

As they stood there, Steve couldn't shake the feeling that they were being watched. Time was slipping away, and with each clue, the mystery deepened, pulling them further into its web.

They started looking for anything that resembled a broken bell or a bird's statue.

As they passed through a grassy area, the ground beneath them suddenly gave way, and they felt themselves plummeting down. They landed with a thud at the bottom of a concealed pit, surrounded by the smell of damp earth and the sound of rustling leaves.

Rubbing their scratched arms, they looked up to see two figures peering down at them, their faces lit with smug satisfaction. One of them leaned over the edge, a smirk playing on his lips. "You think you can win this game?" the he taunted, glancing at the others with a mix of arrogance and disdain. "We've set traps for everyone who thinks they can get ahead of us."

The second figure chimed in, chuckling darkly, "Enjoy your little trip to the pit while we claim the prize. Good luck getting out!" With that, they disappeared from view, leaving Steve, Lexi, and Lucas in the dim light of the pit.

Steve's heart raced. "Great, just what we needed. We're not just racing against time; we're competing against these maniacs!" He looked at Lexi, who seemed unfazed, her expression distant as if lost in thought.

Lucas frowned; frustration evident on his face. "So much for a friendly treasure hunt. What do we do now?"

"First, we need to figure out how deep this pit is and if there's a way out,"

Lexi replied, scanning the walls. "And then we need to find a way to turn the tables on those two."

As they sat in the pit, Steve glanced around, searching for something they could use. "Look, there are some sturdy stems over there!" he pointed.

"Let's gather as many as we can," Lexi urged, her voice urgent.

They scrambled to collect the stems, working quickly. "If we braid them together, it should hold our weight," Lucas suggested, demonstrating how to twist the stems together.

Finally, after a few tense minutes of tying knots, they created a makeshift rope. Lexi tugged at it to test its strength. "I think it'll hold!"

"Only one way to find out," Lucas said, looking up at the top of the pit. "On three?"

"Let's do it!" Steve exclaimed, adrenaline pumping through him.

As they climbed out, breathless and dirty, Steve paused at the top, glancing back at the pit. "That was way too close for comfort," he said, wiping sweat from his brow.

Lexi let out a shaky laugh. "Who knew a treasure hunt could be this dangerous?"

Lucas shook his head, half-smiling. "I can't believe those two set that trap. They think they can win by cheating?"

"Let's keep moving," Steve urged, his voice steadying. "We can't let them get ahead of us."

They asked around and eventually came across an old school building that was not functioning currently. The bell in the front yard was broken and beside it was a letter box and top of it, statue of a bird. Steve looked at the hourglass, it was almost to the end. They saw the two maniacs from earlier rushing toward the school.

Without a warning, Lucas ran toward the school with a burst of speed that surprised everyone. He reached the letter box just seconds before their rivals. Steve and Lexi reached just in time to see that inside the letterbox was another folded note and a small, neatly gift-wrapped box. Just as Steve was about to pull them out, the man who had been making announcements earlier approached with a wide grin.

"Well done! You've won the hunt!" he declared, a sense of satisfaction in his voice. "Hope you enjoyed the mysterious letter as well—it sure caused a lot of buzz!" He winked, oblivious to their confused stares.

"Mysterious letter?" Lexi asked, narrowing her eyes.

"Yeah, the one we left at all the hotel and house doors to kick off the treasure hunt," he said casually, as other participants started making their way toward the school.

Steve's heart dropped. The mysterious letter wasn't some cryptic clue leading to a darker truth. It was just part of the game. They stood there, frozen in place as the man wandered off, congratulating other groups.

Lexi was the first to speak, her voice tinged with disbelief. "So ... all this time, we were chasing after some... game?"

They hastily unfolded the final note, desperate for clarity, but the words on the page hit them like a cruel joke: *'The real treasure is the memories we make along the way.'* Steve's grip tightened, his pulse quickening in frustration. This couldn't be it. Not after everything they'd been through.

"There has to be more," he muttered, almost pleading. His gaze fell on the gift box.

They opened it, and inside was a shiny watch with a gleaming dial and bright leather straps.

"Maybe there's something hidden," Lexi said, though her tone was uncertain now. "Behind the dial or engraved in the leather?"

They hurried to inspect the watch, separating the parts, their hopes dwindling with every second. But there was nothing—no hidden message, no secret compartment. Just a regular watch.

"So much for finding the babies.", Lucas remarked, clearly directed at Lexi.

They stood there, the watch still in Steve's hands, the weight of disappointment sinking into their bones. Lexi shook her head, staring at the note. "This can't be it. There has to be more."

Before Steve could reply, he felt the slightest tremor beneath his feet. A distant rumble echoed through the air. Lexi's eyes went wide. "Did you hear that?"

Steve turned towards the direction of the sound. Another rumble, closer this time. And then— **Boom.**

The ground shook violently. Screams erupted in the distance as a cloud of dust billowed into the air. Steve stumbled, gripping the watch tightly as he tried to stay on his feet. Lucas cursed, looking around, eyes wild with panic.

"What the hell just happened?"

Before anyone could move, a sharp tug pulled at Steve's chest, like an invisible hand yanking him backward. His vision blurred, and the world spun out of control. The explosion, the chaos, the people—it all began to fade. With a dizzying rush, Steve and Lucas were thrown back into the familiar darkness. The loud explosion was replaced by the eerie silence of the library.

Dusty bookshelves loomed over them, and the dim light from the high windows flickered as if the building itself was trying to catch its breath. Steve staggered, trying to regain his footing. Lucas, beside him, clutched his head, groaning in confusion. Steve's pulse raced as he glanced at his hand, half-expecting the watch to be gone—but no. It was still there, ticking silently, as if mocking him. "Back here again..." Lucas muttered under his breath; eyes wide with disbelief. "What was that?"

CHAPTER FOURTEEN

DÉJÀ VU

"Do you think Lexi will be alright?" Steve asked, his heart still pounding from the explosion. His voice cracked with worry.

"She'll be fine, mate," Lucas muttered, rubbing his temples, trying to shake off the disorientation. "But that explosion... it didn't feel like part of the game. What do you think it means?"

"I don't know," Steve said, pacing, tension tightening his chest. "If the scavenger hunt was just a game, how does the explosion fit into it?"

"First bullets, now this," Lucas continued, his voice trembling slightly. "What if this is more dangerous than we thought?"

Steve hesitated, glancing back toward the empty space where they had been pulled away. "We need to get the next clue fast. I want to make sure Lexi's okay."

Lucas frowned. "Shouldn't we rest a bit? You know, take a minute to breathe after nearly getting blown up?"

"We don't have time for that," Steve shot back, frustration lacing his words. "We need to find Lexi, now."

Lucas held his gaze, a mix of weariness and fear in his eyes. "I'm not sure running after the next clue is the best idea, Steve. What if we're just walking into more danger?"

"Danger or not," Steve said firmly, his jaw clenched. "I'm not leaving her alone."

For the first time since their journey began, Steve felt an odd eagerness to part with one of his memories. The urgency to ensure Lexi's safety drowned out any hesitation.

His mind raced as he searched for a memory to trade, finally settling on one that had once filled him with pride—a memory of winning a competition and receiving a gold medal. His parents had been so proud, beaming as they brought him his favourite dinner that night. He remembered the warmth of his parents' smiles, their voices filled with pride as they praised him, the taste of the dinner, rich and comforting. But now, the memory faded into a void. But the ache was quickly swallowed by his mounting concern for Lexi.

The usual emptiness left behind by a traded memory was overrun by an avalanche of emotions—concern, fear, and something that felt uncomfortably close to love. As soon as the next clue appeared in his hands, his heart raced. He didn't even pause to absorb the details. There was no time. Without a second thought, he sprinted toward the library, his only focus on finding Lexi.

This new memory felt like déjà vu. They were standing in a busy street—the same one where they had first met Lexi. The buzzing vehicles and throngs of people around them felt strangely familiar. A girl in her late twenties was walking towards them, her beauty breathtaking. Long, golden hair shimmered in the light, framing her delicate face, and her large, sapphire-blue eyes held an innocent depth that seemed almost unnatural. Dressed in a flowing pastel gown, she moved with an elegance that made her seem otherworldly. She stopped before them and fixed her gaze on Steve.

"Jeff, how come you're here? I told you I'd be safe.", she said in a determined tone.

Steve's mind went blank. Confusion flickered across his face as he exchanged a glance with Lucas. Why did this feel like a re-enactment?

Before he could respond, a waitress rushed up to the girl, handing her a purse she had left behind in a restaurant.

As the girl took it, a piece of paper fluttered from her hand and instinctively, Steve bent to pick it up.

His heart skipped a beat—it was the same bill, with Lexi's name on it. None of this made sense. Who was this girl? Why was this memory repeating itself with puzzling differences? All Steve knew was that this girl looked familiar, like a face he should remember but couldn't quite place. The girl took her purse, thanked the waitress, and turned her piercing gaze back to Steve.

"Well, I'm still waiting for an answer, Jeff." Her voice was calm yet expectant.

Hearing 'Jeff' this time felt different, as if the name belonged to him.

Suddenly, a vivid flash came to him—he was in a dimly lit room, and a soft voice was calling out, "Jeff."

He couldn't see her face, but deep down, he knew it was him she was calling. The moment was fleeting, gone as quickly as it had appeared, but the feeling lingered, leaving him disoriented. Before he could understand what the flash meant or think about what to answer the girl, Lucas interrupted.

"Who are you?", he asked the girl.

She shifted her kind yet determined eyes from Steve to Lucas. "I'm Lexi, Jeff's fiancé. We didn't meet yet, have we?" She extended her hand toward him.

He shook her hand in confusion.

But before either of them could make sense of the situation, the girl they believed to be Lexi from the previous memories approached them from the other end.

"Jeff, what are you doing here? You left me alone again after the explosion," she said, annoyance creeping into her voice. Steve turned to her, instantly forgetting the chaos around them. "Are you okay? Are you hurt?" Concern laced his words.

"I'm fine, just a little shaken up from the blast. And who's this girl?" she asked, eyeing the newcomer.

"Jeff, who's she and why is she holding your hand?" the newcomer asked, her tone sharp, a hint of jealousy flashing in her eyes.

"I'm Lexi. Jeff's fiancé," the girl declared, gripping Steve's hand tighter. The newcomer yanked his hand from her grasp and pulled him to her side.

"Don't you dare touch him. He's mine! I'm his fiancé. Jeff, tell her," the newcomer insisted, her arms crossed, her gaze fixed on Steve with an intensity that left him unsettled.

"Yes, Jeff, why don't you tell her who your fiancé is and end this nonsense once and for all? We have more urgent issues to attend to," Lexi interjected, her fingers fidgeting contrasting her sharp and aggressive voice.

Steve stood frozen, uncertainty coursing through him. *I'm not Jeff,* he thought, a wave of panic washing over him. *I'm not anyone's fiancé. Now I have to deal with two girls claiming the same title? This is insane.* His mind raced as he tried to process the chaos around him. Lucas blinked in disbelief; eyes wide with amazement. "So, you're both saying you're Lexi, Jeff's fiancé?"

"Jeff, why do you look so puzzled? How can she be Lexi? She doesn't look anything like me. You and I have known each other since childhood. We've shared moments that are etched into our souls. I thought you'd recognize me even with closed eyes," the newcomer insisted, disbelief lacing her voice.

"You think I just jumped in from nowhere? We've been engaged for a long time now. Jeff will never give my place to anyone else," the other Lexi shot back, her tone defensive.

As Steve listened to their heated exchange, fragments of their past encounters swirled in his mind. Lexi had always seemed evasive, her stories inconsistent.

Her willingness to abandon Lucas in danger, her ignorance of the gang's mark, her cold reaction to her brother's death—all of these moments had felt odd, but he had brushed them off. Now, however, with this new context, they resurfaced, sharper and clearer.

How could this be? Though there had been no deep connection between them, he had always admired her.

He glanced between the two women, his heart racing.

Then he noticed it: the newcomer wore a locket inscribed with the letter 'L'—the same one they had found in their first clue. He had it tucked away in a drawer in the library. Was this merely a coincidence? Or could the newcomer be the real Lexi?

The thought sent a jolt of anger through him. He had given away his memories for what? To be deceived? To be trapped in a loop with sham and distractions?

Steve's frustration boiled over as he turned to Lexi. "Why did you pretend to be her?" His voice was sharp, the accusation hanging heavy in the air. "Why lead us to all those dead ends?"

Lexi looked taken aback, her eyes wide. "But... Jeff... I... No..." she stammered.

"Enough!" Steve's voice cut through the air, sharper than ever before. His heart pounded as his gaze locked on her. "You abandoned Lucas when we were trapped. You didn't even react to your brother's death. And that gang mark—how did you miss it?" His words came out in a torrent, like a flood breaking through a dam. "You've been lying to me this whole time, haven't you?"

Lexi's expression wavered, her confident façade crumbling just slightly. Her eyes filled with tears—tears that Steve had seen too many times to trust now. "No, Jeff, please. You don't understand... I was forced to do this," she said, her voice trembling. "They made me pretend to be her. They said they'd kill me if I didn't play along."

Steve's fists clenched as he heard her words, but he couldn't shake the feeling that something was still off. He glanced at the locket again, and the memory of all the dead ends, all the lies, came rushing back. He couldn't trust her. Not anymore.

"Steve, I'm begging you!" Fake Lexi dropped to her knees, her tears flowing freely now. "I did what I had to do to survive. If I hadn't... who knows what they would have done to me."

She glanced at the real Lexi with a look of pure hatred. "She's part of it too. Don't let her fool you. She's not who you think she is!"

Steve's heart hardened. "No," he said, his voice quieter but firmer than ever before. "I'm done believing your lies."

Steve took a step back, his heart sinking as her grip on his arm slackened. His voice was calm, but his eyes burned with hurt. "You weren't forced into this. You chose to deceive me. And now, it's over."

Lexi's breath hitched; her eyes wide for a moment as she saw the finality in Steve's gaze. But just as quickly, she straightened, her tears vanishing like a mask being removed. She wiped her eyes with a quick swipe, a smirk creeping onto her lips.

"Yeah... who am I kidding?" Her voice, now laced with venom, slithered through the air. "I relished every second, watching you squirm, chasing all the fake clues I planted."

Steve blinked, his chest tightening. "What... why?" The words came out softer than he expected, disbelief seeping into his tone.

"Honestly, I'm amazed you trusted me for this long," she said, tilting her head, her smirk widening. "But then again... I am a wonderful actress."

Steve's brow furrowed, confusion mixing with betrayal. "What did you get out of it?" His voice now edged with anger.

"Oh, me? I was just following orders," she said, her tone light as if they were discussing the weather. "But I do hope you enjoyed my little performance."

Before Steve could react, Lexi spun on her heel and disappeared into the crowd, her mocking laughter echoing in his ears.

Steve stood rooted to the spot, his mind racing. Who was she really? And more importantly—who had given her those orders?

The real Lexi hugged him tightly, almost desperately, as if afraid to let go. "I'm glad this is over," she murmured, relief evident in her voice. But even as Steve felt her soft hands around him, he couldn't shake the lingering feelings for the fake Lexi. How could he trust the real Lexi completely when the fake one had stirred genuine emotions within him?

As he glanced at Lucas, he found him watching the scene with a bemused expression, amusement flickering in his eyes, unaware of the storm brewing within Steve.

CHAPTER FIFTEEN

THE TRUE TRAIL

After the shock of fake Lexi's betrayal began to wear off, Steve found his voice again. Deep down, he knew he had no choice but to press on—to find the real girl he'd been searching for all along. Despite the anger and frustration simmering within him, he forced himself to focus and turned to the real Lexi. "So, what's the plan?" he asked, trying to mask his weariness.

Lexi's expression was calm, her voice steady but firm. "I've got intel that the gang might be operating in this city. I came to confirm it myself."

Steve hoped this wasn't another wild goose chase. His body screamed for rest, exhaustion tugging at his every muscle, but he couldn't afford to quit now. Swallowing his doubts, he nodded. "Alright. Let's look for the clue."

As they walked toward the bus stop, a group of children caught their attention—begging by the roadside, their clothes torn, bodies smeared with grime.

But something about them seemed off. Their wide, nervous eyes darted around, as if expecting danger at any moment. Fear clung to them like a shadow.

Lexi crouched down and asked gently, "What's wrong?" But the children wouldn't speak. They just kept scanning their surroundings, trembling.

Steve and Lucas approached, and as Steve knelt to speak to one of the boys, his gaze fell on something that sent a chill down his spine. On the boy's arm was a mark—faint but unmistakable: a skull with two crossed bones. The same symbol that had haunted them at every turn. His heart quickened as he checked the other children. Each of them bore the same symbol, carved deep into their skin.

Steve could only imagine the agony they had endured to bear such a mark, the cruel permanence of it searing into their flesh. Steve nudged Lexi, drawing her attention to the mark. Lucas saw it too, and the three of them exchanged knowing glances. This was it—the first solid lead they'd uncovered since the start of their journey. These children were their link to the culprits.

Without wasting time, they led the kids to a nearby restaurant. At first, the children hesitated, casting suspicious glances at the strangers, but Lexi's gentle tone and reassuring presence slowly put them at ease. They ate as though they hadn't seen food in days, their small hands clutching the plates, shovelling each bite with a quiet desperation. Afterward, they bought the children clean clothes from a nearby shop and took them back to Lexi's motel. There, they helped them wash up, scrubbing away the grime and dirt, revealing skin marred by fear and the cruel mark they all bore. Once dressed in fresh clothes, the children looked less fragile, and their guarded expressions began to soften. By the end of it all, the children were no longer silent. They looked at Steve, Lexi, and Lucas with trust in their eyes, ready—finally—to talk.

The children spoke hesitantly at first, their voices trembling as they recounted their lives. They told them of a large room made of stones and cloth where they and many others like them were kept.

They ate only once a day—just bread and jam—before being sent out to beg on the streets, forced to hand over every coin to their masters. They had never seen their masters' faces.

The men always wore masks, their identities hidden behind a veil of cruelty.

As the children spoke of these masked figures, their fear was palpable. They admitted they were beaten savagely if they didn't bring back enough money. The more they spoke, the more their small bodies trembled, memories of years of abuse breaking through their fragile composure.

They were just children, children who should have been running carefree with friends instead of enduring this nightmare. Steve, Lucas, and Lexi exchanged silent looks of deep concern. None of them deserved the fate that had been carved into their skin.

The children gave them a vague idea of where the hideout was but were too terrified to return. So, Lucas stayed behind with the kids at the motel, while Lexi and Steve prepared to investigate.

"Shouldn't we involve the police? We might need backup," Steve suggested, glancing at her.

"I tried," Lexi replied, her voice edged with frustration. "But they said they have more important cases to solve than chasing a cold trail."

"So, we're on our own, huh?" Steve asked, his tone resigned.

Lexi gave a confident smile. "Don't worry, Jeff. Remember? I'm a witch—I'll handle them."

As they set out toward the gang's suspected hideout, Steve found himself staring at her for a moment, trying to push away the mix of emotions bubbling beneath the surface. He was determined not to let his guard down again, still reeling from the sting of recent betrayal.

Yet, there was something about this Lexi. Ever since meeting her, strange flashes had begun to invade his mind. Some were just disembodied voices, calling him Jeff. Others were of a man and a woman together, spending quality time. He couldn't see their faces, but the feeling of familiarity was undeniable, as if these fragments were pieces of a forgotten part of his life. Each time the visions came, they grew a little clearer, offering him brief moments of peace, like whispers of a past that was slowly surfacing.

They arrived at the area the children had described, and it was exactly as bleak as they'd imagined.

The streets were lined with rundown buildings, their windows cracked or boarded up, but there was no sign of the warmth or vibrancy of a typical neighbourhood. Instead, the streets were filled with rough-looking people, each one eyeing them with a cold, hostile glare. The tension in the air was thick, as if a single wrong move could spark a confrontation.

Steve felt his pulse quicken as they moved deeper into the maze of narrow lanes. "There are so many buildings. How are we supposed to find the right one?" he whispered; his voice tight with urgency. "These people don't look like they're going to be much help."

Lexi glanced around, her eyes scanning the area. "I don't know," she admitted softly. "But let's keep moving. We'll look for any place that matches the kids' description—stone and cloth. It's all we've got." There was a glimmer of determination in her voice, even though the odds seemed stacked against them.

As they walked, Steve and Lexi accidentally bumped into a burly man. His eyes flashed with rage, and he looked ready to strike when Lexi quickly muttered an apology, pulling Steve along before anything could escalate. They moved swiftly, hearts pounding, navigating the maze-like streets for what felt like ten minutes before they reached a secluded area, hidden by a thick canopy of trees. The air felt heavier here, as if this place wasn't meant to be found.

There, nestled among the trees, was the building—the one made of stone and cloth, just as the children had described. Steve's heart leapt with a mix of anticipation and dread. But as they moved toward it, a hand shot out from the shadows, yanking them back into the cover of the trees. Startled, they turned to face an elderly man, small and wiry, his bald head gleaming faintly in the dappled sunlight filtering through the leaves.

"What are you doing here?" the man asked in a low, urgent whisper. "This place... it's dangerous. You won't leave in one piece if you step inside."

"Who are you?" Lexi asked, her tone cautious, every muscle in her body on alert.

"Doesn't matter," he replied cryptically. "Just think of me as a well-wisher. Dark things happen here. Horrors that will make you choke on your own screams. Turn back—before it's too late."

Steve, having learned hard lessons about trusting strangers, narrowed his eyes. "Thanks for the warning, Mr. Well-Wisher," he said, his voice edged with sarcasm, "but we can take care of ourselves."

Lexi gave Steve a look and turned to the man, "Sir, we appreciate your concern for us but we're here to help the children. We have to rescue them and end the horror that etched this place for so long.", her voice was gentle and kind.

"Don't say I didn't warn you," the man muttered before slipping into the shadows, disappearing as mysteriously as he had appeared.

Steve glanced at the hourglass, its presence now feeling more ominous than ever. The sand continued to trickle down, each grain marking the relentless passage of time. It had become their silent, unforgiving companion.

He knew that if they didn't find a clue soon, time would run out—and the consequences of that were terrifyingly unknown. Would they be pulled back to the library once more? Or, worse, trapped in this memory forever?

They moved cautiously toward the old building, every step careful, avoiding the crunch of dried leaves beneath their feet. Lexi was a few steps ahead of him, her movements swift and determined. But just as Steve prepared to follow, he felt it—that familiar, gut-wrenching pull. In an instant, the world around him blurred, and before he could even process it, he was back in the old library, standing beside Lucas. He instantly noticed that the library was drenched in darkness once again.

CHAPTER SIXTEEN

THE PLAN

"Not now!" Steve snapped, kicking a chair hard enough to send it skidding across the floor. "We need to save the kids, and we don't even know where the next memory will take us." He clenched his fists. "I just hope Lexi can handle things alone."

"Only one way to find out," Lucas said with a shrug, though his eyes were tense.

They quickly went to complete the memory exchange for their next clue. Steve hesitated. The memory flickered in his mind—Thanksgiving dinner when he was seven. The smell of turkey, Charlie's squeals of joy, their parents' smiles as they handed out gifts. It was perfect, a memory he'd clung to.

As a shimmer in the air, the soul barely needed to touch Steve for the memory to transfer. It rippled, pulsating with energy as the fragment of Steve's life was drawn in. To the soul, this was a simple transaction, its form bending and twisting as it absorbed the memory into its endless archive. It vibrated briefly, acknowledging the trade. "Another piece for the land," it murmured, more to itself than to Steve. The soul had no attachment to the memory, only to its role as the custodian of this strange place.

Fortunately, the next memory brought them back to where they had left off. Lucas was in the motel room with the children, while Steve stayed close behind Lexi. He let out a sigh of relief—she was still moving cautiously ahead, her eyes scanning every inch of their surroundings. They crept forward until they reached the last tree bordering the house, and ducked behind it. Steve peered out from behind the tree.

Three burly masked men stood guard at the front door, guns in hand, their faces hidden but their postures tense.

Through the dusty windows, faint shadows flickered inside. He couldn't tell whether the shapes belonged to the children or more goons. Steve's heart pounded. They needed a plan. With a silent nod to Lexi, they carefully retraced their steps, slipping back into the trees until they were far enough to speak without being overheard.

"How are we supposed to get inside without being caught? We don't even have any weapons," Steve said, tension rising in his voice.

"I knew we couldn't just barge in," Lexi replied, her eyes gleaming with determination. "I've come up with a plan on the way here." Her gaze met his, intense and unwavering. "But we'll have only one chance, and we'll need to move quickly. There won't be time to second-guess once we're inside."

It sounded like an impossible task, but with no other options left, Steve took a breath and asked, "What's the plan?"

"I'll create a distraction for the guards," she explained, her voice calm, as if outlining a well-rehearsed strategy. "But not all of them might leave. So, I'll cast an invisibility spell on us—it should let us slip past unnoticed." Her tone was methodical, like a teacher repeating a lesson to a struggling student. "But that's only the easy part."

Steve's brow furrowed. "Easy part?"

"The real trick is inside. The spells won't last long, and we have no idea how many goons are waiting or where the children are being held, assuming they're even there." Lexi's words hung in the air, heavy with uncertainty.

"Lot of ifs and buts," Steve muttered, his apprehension deepening.

"Now, we want to avoid confrontation at all costs," Lexi said firmly. "Our primary goal is to rescue the children. We'll deal with the goons later."

"Aye aye, captain!" Steve quipped, though his grin faded quickly as the gravity of the situation set in.

"Once we enter, we'll split up to search the building—faster that way. Look for any locked doors, hidden rooms, anything that seems off."

"And if everything goes perfectly, we grab the kids and get out unnoticed," Steve said, raising an eyebrow. "Sounds a bit... impossible."

Lexi nodded; her face serious. "Yes, which is why I have backup plans." Her tone left no room for debate.

Steve glanced at her, impressed despite himself. "You thought of all this in the short time we've been here?" he asked, his voice tinged with disbelief.

For a second, Lexi blushed at the praise, but quickly snapped back into her no-nonsense demeanour. "Here's how it works. If the invisibility spell starts to wear off, we hide—use anything we can find to stay out of sight. If we get spotted, we call for backup. I can use my powers to hold them off while you find the children."

Steve shook his head, the doubt in his voice unmistakable. "It's risky. Too many unknowns. Do you think we'll actually pull this off?"

Lexi met his gaze, her expression unwavering. "We have to," she said quietly. "There's no other choice."

"Just one more thing," Lexi added, her voice firm. "If we find the kids and the guards catch on before we can escape, I'll stall them. You take the kids to safety."

Steve opened his mouth to protest, but Lexi cut him off sharply. "This is why I'm telling you now, Jeff. We won't have time for arguments when things go south. Promise me—if it comes to that, you'll take the kids and go. No hesitation."

His heart pounded at the thought of leaving her behind.

Reluctantly, Steve nodded, but his worried gaze lingered on her face.

Seeing his unease, Lexi softened for a moment. "I'll be fine, Jeff," she said gently. "I made a vow to stay with you forever, and I'll keep it. No matter what happens. You have to trust me."

"And if anything unexpected happens, we'll have to think fast. The kids are our priority," Lexi added, her voice steady.

He couldn't help but notice the stark contrast between the two Lexis: One who was willing to leave a friend in danger to save herself and the other one who is ready to sacrifice herself for children she doesn't even know.

Steve nodded, but just as he did, another flash hit him. He was at a beach, sitting with a girl who leaned against his shoulder. He couldn't see her face, but her hand was wrapped tightly around his. Her voice was soft but certain. "Jeff, I promise I'll never leave you. You and me—we're forever. I promise."

Before he could make sense of it, the vision vanished.

Lexi's concerned voice cut through his daze. "What's wrong, Jeff?"

He blinked, forcing himself back to reality. There was no time to get lost in memories, no matter how unsettling. They had a mission. "Nothing," he said, clearing his throat. "Just a bit nervous, I guess."

THE RESCUE

They exchanged a final nod before Lexi created a diversion for the guards. She conjured an illusion of the children running into the woods on the right side of the building. When the guards noticed, they rushed toward the illusion, and one guard went inside, likely to check on the children.

"This is our chance!" Lexi urged, casting the invisibility spell over them. Steve noticed her hand trembling slightly, but when he asked, she brushed it off. "I hope that guard went in to check on the children. If we follow him, we'll reach them soon."

They hurried to the main door, but just before entering, Lexi stopped him and cast another spell. "What's that for?" Steve asked. "It's a protection charm—a shield to keep you safe." As she spoke the final words, Lexi stumbled, her energy visibly drained.

Steve knelt beside her. "Lexi, what's going on?"

"Maintaining three spells is exhausting me, but we don't have time," she insisted, struggling to stand. Before he could protest, Lexi pushed forward, stepping inside, though Steve could see the toll it was taking on her.

They could hear footsteps echoing below. Moving swiftly but silently, they followed the sound until they reached a narrow staircase descending into darkness. With hearts pounding, they carefully stepped down, noting the crumbling and the shaky walls, worn steps that looked ready to collapse at any moment. The spiral staircase seemed endless, winding down in dizzying circles as the sound of footsteps stayed just out of reach.

Finally, they reached a half-open door at the base of the staircase.

With a shared look of determination, they slipped through without hesitation.

They found themselves in yet another corridor with turns, empty and foreboding, with no visible doors or exits.

Following the faint sound of footsteps, they moved forward—only to reach a dead end.

The footsteps continued, just ahead, but there was no sign of an opening.

They exchanged a look of silent frustration, each unsure of what to do next. Just then, Lexi's eyes caught on a barely visible lever on the wall, cleverly camouflaged to escape notice. She pressed it with a hopeful breath, and, with a low rumble, the wall shifted, revealing a hidden passageway. Without wasting a moment, they resumed their pursuit. But their urgency mounted as they saw the invisibility spell beginning to fade—first their feet, then their legs. They were running out of time.

"I think by now the guards outside must have realized it was just a hoax," Lexi muttered, and Steve nodded grimly. "Which means we're running out of time," he added, his voice taut. The corridor led them to a heavy door just as the guard they'd been following was locking it, grumbling to himself. Lexi and Steve quickly ducked behind a pillar, holding their breath. Fortunately, the guard was too preoccupied, heading straight to the hidden wall without a second glance.

The moment he disappeared, they hurried to the door, only to find it locked.

Steve's heart sank—this lock looked impenetrable, as though it had once guarded something of great importance.

"Now what?" he whispered, frustration seeping into his tone.

Lexi smirked softly. "You keep forgetting that I'm a witch."

"No, you already look drained. I won't let you use any more magic," he insisted, his gaze full of worry. But Lexi shook her head, determined. "I'm fine, Jeff. Remember what we agreed—no hesitation."

Without waiting for his reply, Lexi raised her trembling hand, drawing on her last reserves of strength. The lock clicked open, as though guided by an invisible hand.

Lexi swayed, looking more exhausted than ever, but she steadied herself, nodding to Steve. They slipped inside, and what they saw made their blood run cold. In the centre of the dimly lit room, a group of children huddled together, bound tightly with ropes that bit cruelly into their skin.

They were pale and malnourished, looking just as fragile as the ones they had seen before.

Gags muffled their voices, and their clothes were little more than torn rags. Their eyes, wide and filled with fear, locked onto Lexi and Steve, silently pleading for help. Steve clenched his fists, feeling a surge of both anger and determination. There was no turning back now.

They moved swiftly, untying the children and gently removing their gags. The children still looked terrified, eyes darting around, not quite believing they were safe. Lexi knelt beside them, her voice soft and reassuring. "Don't be afraid; we're here to help. We'll get you out of here."

Steve and Lexi guided the children carefully through the dim corridor, past the hidden lever, and down the winding staircase. The atmosphere was tense; every creak and whisper of movement made their hearts race. So far, they hadn't encountered anyone, but as they reached the entrance hall, hushed voices floated in from outside.

They peered around the corner and saw three guards, deep in conversation. "The boss would have killed us if we'd lost them," one grumbled.

"Yeah, but what was all that about anyway? Children running away? We searched everywhere and saw nothing," replied another, scratching his head.

"Let's stay sharp, just in case," suggested a third guard, though the first one dismissed him with a wave. "They're tied up and gagged. What could they possibly do?"

The guards continued their conversation, unaware of the tense scene unfolding just a few feet away.

"The children who were on duty should have returned by now," the third guard grumbled.

"It's not like they have anywhere to run, or the brains to think of it," the second one retorted.

Steve and Lexi exchanged a quick look, realizing the guards were referring to the children they'd already managed to rescue. They had no time to lose. Scanning the room, they searched frantically for a back exit—only to find none. The main door was their only way out.

Suddenly, a quiet cough escaped from one of the children. Steve and Lexi's eyes widened as the guards shot each other alarmed looks.

"Did you hear that?" the third guard whispered, eyes narrowing. "It sounded like a cough."

"Go check it out, Henry," the first guard ordered.

As the second guard started toward them, the group fell silent, tension tightening around them like a vice. They held their breath, frozen in place. They were seconds away from being discovered.

As the guard entered the hall, his eyes swept across the room, searching for any sign of movement. He furrowed his brow, scanning once more, but found nothing. With a frustrated grunt, he turned back to his friends. "Nothing here.", he shouted to his friends outside.

Inside the wooden box beside the stairs, the children let out a collective sigh of relief. Steve had found the hiding spot just in time, and the narrow escape only heightened their sense of urgency.

Lexi and Steve were engaged in a heated argument about their escape route when a child among them spoke up, his voice trembling with fear.

"One time, I heard the goons talking," he said, glancing around as if expecting the shadows to spring to life. "They were saying something about a secret exit."

Lexi knelt down to his level, her hand resting gently on his shoulder. "What exactly did they say? Do you remember?"

The boy nodded; his eyes wide with the weight of his memories. "They said they'd use it when the grand plan was executed." Lexi exchanged a worried glance with Steve, dread creeping into their hearts. A 'grand plan'? What horrors awaited these innocent souls?

"We need to find that door as soon as possible," Steve urged, his voice sharp with urgency. "You stay here with the kids while I look for any hidden levers like we found before."

"Be careful," Lexi whispered, watching him with worry as he slipped into the shadows. Each step he took felt heavy with the risk of discovery, and the silence in the corridor deepened, amplifying the pounding of their hearts. She could feel the tension mounting as time slipped away, aware that every second brought them closer to the guards' realization that the children were missing.

Steve felt the weight of the moment bearing down on him—the urgency, the task at hand; it was unnerving. He silently scanned the walls of the hall, searching for anything that might reveal a hidden door. Each inch of the rough stone surface yielded no clues as he tapped and felt along, desperate for a lever or a hidden mechanism. But nothing.

As he moved, he accidentally tripped over something, the sudden noise making him hold his breath, praying the guards hadn't heard. For nearly half an hour, he scoured the hall, but his efforts were met with frustration.

Desperation gnawed at him as he decided to stealthily ascend to the first floor, hoping for better luck. Seconds turned into agonizing minutes, yet he found no signs of an escape route.

Just as he was about to turn back, another flash struck him. This time, he saw a girl, blindfolded, playfully trying to catch someone. Her laughter filled the air with warmth and joy.

With a sudden jolt, he realized that she was trying to catch him—and for the first time, he could see her face clearly.

His heart raced as he recognized her: it was Lexi! How could he be seeing something that never happened? The vision faded, leaving him bewildered, but there was no time to dwell on it.

With a heavy heart, he made his way back to their hiding place. "There's no escape route." he said, his voice filled with disappointment.

Just then, one of the kids tried to stand up, his legs cramped from crouching too long. He reached for the bottom of the box for support but lost his grip and slipped. The sudden movement caused the bottom to slide slightly. Lexi's eyes widened as she noticed the shift and quickly investigated. To her astonishment, she found a lever concealed beneath the box!

"Everyone, move out of the box!" she urged, her heart racing with hope. As the kids scrambled out, Lexi pressed the lever, and to their surprise, the bottom of the box slid aside, revealing a hidden staircase descending into darkness.

"I thought the box was too large, but I didn't expect this," Steve exclaimed, a flicker of excitement igniting his spirits.

"And you were searching everywhere else!" Lexi shot back, a grin breaking through the tension.

Hoping the staircase would lead them to freedom, they descended cautiously. Lexi brought up the rear, ensuring that each child made it down safely. The staircase was short, with few turns; it opened into an abandoned tunnel designed for crossing roads. One by one, the children scrambled down, their faces a mix of fear and hope.

As the last child reached the bottom, they all turned their eyes expectantly toward the entrance, waiting for Lexi to follow. Minutes passed, stretching into an eternity, and still, there was no sign of her. A knot of worry tightened in Steve's stomach. He wanted to rush back, to check on her, but he remembered the promise he had made: to lead the children to safety, no matter the cost.

With a heavy heart, he steeled himself against the dread coiling in his chest.

Whispering reassurances to the frightened kids, he guided them deeper into the tunnel, hoping against hope that Lexi would find her way back to them.

As they moved forward, he glanced back one last time, wishing for her swift return before plunging into the unknown.

CHAPTER EIGHTEEN

THE CAPTURE

Steve hurriedly ushered the children back to the motel room, his mind racing with worry about Lexi. He was just about to turn back when something unexpected happened. Without warning, he and Lucas were yanked back into the familiar setting of the library, the familiar dizziness washing over them as reality shifted.

As soon as they steadied themselves, Lucas grabbed his shoulder, his voice filled with alarm. "I just got a call from the village," he said, barely able to contain his urgency. "Someone kidnapped Oliver. They said if we want Lexi and Oliver alive, we have to return the children."

Steve's eyes widened. "Oliver? You mean the same man who was tied and gagged in the first memory we visited?"

"Looks like it," Lucas replied, confusion mingling with worry. "Could that first memory be tied to this one somehow?"

Steve shook his head, the urgency overriding any chance to unravel the mystery. "I don't know, but we don't have time to figure it out. We need to go back—now!" With that, he spun around and bolted toward the exit, desperation propelling him forward.

Steve exchanged the memory of the day he received his horses—a gift from a wealthy man in gratitude for his help. He remembered how he had been captivated by the horses at first sight, and how Charlie's excitement had been boundless, bouncing with joy as the horses looked back at him with almost human amusement. As the memory faded, Lucas observed him with a curious, probing gaze.

"You're missing something, aren't you?" Lucas asked, a hint of intrigue in his voice as he watched Steve, whose movements seemed subtly disjointed, as if some essential part of him hadn't fully arrived with them.

Without dwelling on the empty feeling, they opened the door to their next memory and found themselves back in the motel room, surrounded by the children. Steve didn't hesitate. "Lucas, take these kids back to the village and hide them at Lexi's house until I get back with her and Oliver."

Lucas raised an eyebrow, concerned. "But won't the goons head straight there to look for them?"

"No," Steve replied confidently. "It's the last place they'd check—too obvious to be suspicious."

Lucas nodded, a hint of admiration in his gaze. "Smart thinking." With that, they parted ways, each aware of the stakes, each moving toward a piece of the unknown puzzle ahead.

Steve hurried back to the building where they'd rescued the children earlier. To his surprise, the entrance was deserted; no guards, no sign of movement.

He slipped inside, checking each room and corridor, but found nothing but silence and emptiness.

He reached the spot near the box they'd escaped from earlier, and to his surprise, Lexi's locket, the one with the letter L inscribed on it, lay on the floor. Picking it up, his tension mounted as the significance of this discovery hit him. Doubt gnawed at him—was there another hidden room he'd missed? After another sweep of the place, still finding nothing, he stepped outside, scanning the area in frustration.

Just as he was about to turn back, something caught his eye—a faint, almost forgotten trail of wet sand, winding off into the shadows.

With cautious steps, he followed the path, which twisted through thickening trees.

He pressed on, losing track of direction and time, the silence around him growing heavy.

Then, as the trees began to thin again, he sensed movement—a shadow, too late. A sudden, sharp blow struck the back of his head, and the world spun into darkness as he fell to the ground, his last thoughts a blur of alarm.

Steve's head throbbed from the earlier blow as he began to stir.

Slowly, he realized he was lying on the ground, tightly bound and gagged.

He didn't know how long he was unconscious. He tried to shift his weight but found himself immobilized. Faint voices drifted nearby, too garbled to make sense. He called out, his muffled voice barely escaping, but desperation drove him to keep trying. Just as hope began to fade, he heard footsteps approaching, quick and purposeful. Two figures rushed over, hastily untying him. Though they looked strikingly familiar, he couldn't make out their face in the shadows.

As soon as his hands were free, he bolted toward the direction of the voices, not pausing to thank his rescuers. Lexi's locket slipped from his pocket and hit the ground unnoticed in his hurry. Ahead, the outline of an old warehouse loomed. Just then, a strange thought flashed through his mind—*Had he somehow saved himself in that first memory?* But he shook it off; there was no time to unravel that mystery now.

He sprinted toward the warehouse he'd spotted earlier and paused just outside. It looked familiar—the same one from their previous memory.

A strong feeling told him that Oliver was somewhere inside. But where was Lexi? His eyes scanned the surrounding area, and soon enough, he noticed another warehouse hidden in shadows of the trees.

Heart pounding, he ran to it and found an old, rusted window. Peeking inside, he saw that the warehouse interior was cloaked in a thick layer of dust and grime, the air dense with the smell of rust and decay.

Cobwebs hung in heavy sheets from the rafters, casting strange, twisted shadows across the room. Faint creaks echoed from above, as though the building itself were alive, watching, waiting. Steve felt his pulse quicken as he leaned in closer, each nerve on edge, straining to pick up any sound that might give away Lexi's whereabouts.

And then he saw it; there in the centre of the room, Lexi was tied to a metal rod, gagged and unconscious. Two men stood guard nearby.

"Boss will be here soon," one of the guards muttered, glancing nervously toward the door. "And he won't be happy if we mess this up like last time. You know what he did to the last guy who crossed him."

"Yeah," the other replied, shivering slightly. "After today, no one's ever going to forget this place...or what he's planning."

Just then, a man with a lean frame entered the room, but his face was obscured in the dim light. Steve strained to see through the murky darkness, frustration gnawing at him. He could barely make out the boss's outline, and the sense of helplessness stirred a knot of anger and dread in his chest. The guards straightened at his arrival. "Welcome, boss," one greeted, though the man ignored him.

"Wake her up," he ordered. One of the guards splashed water on Lexi's face. She blinked slowly, her expression shifting from groggy confusion to shock in an instant. Her eyes widened as she focused on the man before her, and she gasped, "YOU!"

CHAPTER NINETEEN

A STARTLING REVELATION

"I'm so glad you came! Please help me!" Lexi pleaded, desperation and trust shining in her eyes. The man's response was a dark, sardonic laugh that made her blood run cold.

"Help?" he scoffed. "You foolish girl. *I'm* the one who kidnapped you."

Lexi's face went pale. "What? No... That can't be right. You... but you're—how?"

"Oh, I suppose it's safe enough to tell you now, since you won't be around to share it, just like your brother." His voice dropped, each word a venomous whisper. "I was the one behind the disappearing babies."

Outside, Steve's heart pounded as he strained to see through the grimy window. Though the darkness obscured much, the commanding voice was unmistakable—a voice he'd trusted before. It couldn't be true.

This was the man who'd called for the stakeout, the one who'd initiated the search to protect the village... or so Steve thought.

His mind reeled as the revelation crashed over him, disbelief and anger rising.

Inside, Lexi's voice broke through his swirling thoughts, her words laced with horror.

"Liam! How could you?" She choked, her voice trembling with hurt and fury. "What did those innocent babies ever do to you? You saw their mothers crumble, their fathers helpless... and still, none of it moved your heart?"

Liam's mouth twisted into a mocking smile. "Move my heart? What am I—a social worker?" he sneered. "Handling something beyond anyone's imagination was far more exciting than wiping the tears of some fools." His voice dripped with pride and arrogance.

Lexi's voice shook, a raw fury Steve had never heard before. "What did you get out of it?" she demanded, her words trembling with rage.

"Oh, you'd be surprised," Liam replied coolly, amusement flickering in his eyes. "Children bring in quite a fortune when they beg—and that was just the start.

I had grand plans for them, but then you had to interfere and ruin everything. And now you'll pay for it." His voice shifted, frustration simmering beneath the surface.

Outside, Steve's mind raced. He needed to act, and quickly. Every second wasted meant Lexi was one step closer to danger. He clenched his fists, heart pounding with the weight of the choice before him—if he didn't move now, he'd lose her.

He pressed himself into the shadows, his heart pounding as he quickly ran through his options. Then a risky idea came to him. Drawing in a steadying breath, he carefully began mimicking a group of voices calling out from the distance—deep, angry shouts as if a search party was closing in on the warehouse. He layered in whispers and footsteps, just loud enough to create the illusion of a small army moving closer.

The guards exchanged anxious looks, their hands moving to their weapons.

After a tense pause, they glanced around and crept out the side door to investigate the source of the noise, leaving the room momentarily unguarded.

As soon as they were out of sight, Steve slipped through the entrance and hurried toward Lexi, who was bound to a rusted metal pole in the centre of the dimly lit warehouse.

Steve crouched down, his hands working quickly on her restraints. Lexi looked up at him in startled relief, her face pale, but her eyes sharp. She whispered, "Jeff... How did you get in here?" But he shook his head slightly, signalling her to keep quiet as he worked on the ropes.

Just as the last knot loosened, a sudden creak of footsteps echoed from behind him. The guards were returning—quicker than he'd expected. His pulse spiked as he glanced toward the door, realizing their only exit was now blocked. For a split second, he caught Lexi's gaze, and in her eyes, he saw the same grim realization.

He pulled her to her feet, whispering urgently, "Stay behind me." But before they could take even a single step, a voice as cold as steel pierced through the shadows, "Well, well... Look who's come to play hero. Lexi's knight in shining armour."

Steve's blood ran cold at the familiar voice.

It was Liam. A mocking smile tugged at his lips as he stepped into the faint light, his eyes gleaming with twisted amusement. "You really thought you could outsmart me?" He chuckled, the sound dark and menacing. "I knew it was a ruse all along. But now... I have two for the price of one."

Behind him, his goons filtered into the warehouse, blocking every possible exit. Their footsteps echoed ominously, closing in like the tightening grip of a snare. Steve's mind raced as he gauged the numbers, but the odds were grim. Just then, Lexi gathered her strength and, with a desperate look, began whispering an incantation, her hands trembling as she tried to cast a spell. But the earlier magic had drained her, and as she pushed herself beyond her limits, her vision swam, and she stumbled, falling to the floor in exhaustion.

"Lexi!" Steve whispered, grabbing her arm and helping her sit on a nearby chair. His gaze flicked between her and the advancing men. With no other choice, he positioned himself in front of her, fists raised, bracing for the inevitable.

The men advanced with calculated menace, circling him.

He took a swing at the nearest one, and for a brief moment, it looked like he might hold his ground.

But the guards were relentless, their fists and grips overwhelming him. One by one, they forced his defences down until his movements grew sluggish and desperate. With a final shove, they subdued him, pushing him down onto his knees beside Lexi.

Liam stepped forward, smirking as he looked down at both of them, trapped and exhausted. "It's over," he sneered, his voice dripping with triumph.

CHAPTER TWENTY

TRIUMPH

As Liam's goons roughly tied Steve to the rod, a disorienting flash blinds him, pulling him back into a memory he could barely understand. He's in a dimly lit room, breathing hard, struggling as ropes dig into his wrists, just as they are now. Across from him, he sees *Lexi*. They're both in the same trapped, desperate state, tied and helpless, but the Lexi in the memory is trying to comfort him.

"Stay calm, Jeff," her voice echoes through his mind, gentle but resolute, as if this wasn't their first time facing danger together. "We'll get out of this... we always do."

The name *Jeff* jars him, snapping his attention back to the present. *Jeff?* But it's him. He was... Jeff. In another life, with another name, he and Lexi had been through this same terror before, and he had vowed never to let it happen again. But here they were, caught in the same trap, all over again.

The memory fades, but a haunting sense of déjà vu lingers, making him realize: *He was Jeff, and this moment has already played out once.* The intensity of this revelation fills him with renewed determination to break free and protect Lexi.

Lexi's voice trembled, but she managed to ask, "What happens to the newborns you take? We haven't seen them anywhere."

"Oh, those little ones?" Liam replied with a chilling smirk, eyes gleaming with sadistic satisfaction. "I have an orphanage for them, where they're kept until they're...useful to me." He watched her reaction with amusement before his face darkened. "Enough talk. Time for some action."

He nodded to one of his men, who drew a gun, its metallic glint catching the dim light as he levelled it squarely at Lexi's heart. Steve's heart pounded as he struggled against his restraints, yelling desperately, "Leave her alone! Hurt me instead!" But the guard's eyes were cold and unfeeling, his grip on the gun steady and unwavering.

In that moment, the world seemed to freeze, the air thick with impending dread.

Steve's mind raced, his breaths quick and shallow, each one feeling like it might be his last. The guard's finger tightened on the trigger.

A thunderous gunshot shattered the silence. Steve braced for the worst, his eyes widening in terror—only to see blood trickling down the arm of the guard, who staggered back in shock, clutching his wound. Steve's eyes darted beyond, where he spotted police officers surging into the room. Relief flooded through him as he saw Lucas in the distance, a fierce determination in his eyes. The tables had turned! The expression on Liam's face as he was arrested was one of disbelief, as if he couldn't fathom that his seemingly perfect plan had been thwarted.

In moments, they were untied and free. Lucas darted over to Steve, a grin on his face. "I figured you'd need a hand," he said proudly.

"Thanks—I've never been happier to see you," Steve replied with a mischievous smile.

But then, the memory that had hit him while tied up came rushing back, filling him with a sudden sense of revelation.

"Lucas, I finally understand why they all call me Jeffery," he said, his voice thick with wonder.

Lucas raised an eyebrow. "Why?"

"Because I *am* Jeffery. This story—it's mine. Maybe from a past life, but it's still *mine*. It's the only plausible explanation. I don't remember everything but I'm sure, I'm him." Steve's eyes shone, piecing it together aloud. "And do you know what that means?"

Lucas shook his head, marvelling at the spark in Steve's eyes. "What?"

"It means Lexi is *my* fiancée. I don't have to keep holding back my feelings for her." Steve's voice softened, a weight lifting from his heart. "I'd been pulling away, worried about feeling deceived or guilty like before with... the fake Lexi. But with the real Lexi, I don't have to do that. Not anymore."

Just then, Lexi approached, relief shining in her eyes. Steve wrapped her in his arms, holding her close, feeling as though everything, he'd been searching for was finally within reach.

They all thanked the police for their help, sharing the details of Liam's orphanage scheme to ensure every child would be rescued and also about Oliver being held in another warehouse.

From there, they made their way to the village to clear up any lingering fears. That evening, the village came alive with a vibrant celebration. While Liam's betrayal still left a bitter sting, the relief of newfound safety was undeniable.

Lights twinkled in every corner, and the enticing aroma of fresh food wafted through the air, stirring appetites and spirits alike. Villagers danced with abandon; the weight of fear finally lifted.

Steve took Lexi's hand, and they spun through the crowd, his laughter mingling with hers under the night sky. Later, he joined Lucas, and they raised their glasses, sharing a satisfied grin. But just as the glasses touched their lips, the world around them shifted abruptly—they were yanked back into the library, the warmth and sounds of the village disappearing into eerie silence. The library was filled with sunshine once again.

CHAPTER TWENTY-ONE

A TWIST OF FATE

"I wish I could spend more time with her," Steve said, his voice tinged with a rare softness.

"Oh, you will, don't worry," Lucas murmured, almost too quietly.

"What was that?" Steve asked, caught off guard.

"Nothing," Lucas replied quickly, his usual grin resurfacing. "I just meant that maybe you both got your happy ending once upon a time."

"Yeah... maybe," Steve sighed, but something about Lucas's tone pulled him back to the present. "Anyway, we still haven't found the girl I was supposed to find in the first place. We thought solving the mystery of the missing babies would lead to her, but... now what?"

"Come with me," Lucas said, his tone shifting into one Steve had rarely heard from him. "I have something to show you. And bring that key we found in the mirror room—it might come in handy."

For a moment, Steve hesitated. There was a new weight in Lucas's voice, an authority that felt foreign. He couldn't shake the feeling that something in their dynamic had just shifted, something he couldn't quite put his finger on.

Steve trailed behind Lucas; their silence thick with an unspoken tension. There was a new determination in

Lucas's stride, a sharpness that Steve had never seen before. They passed several familiar buildings, winding deeper into alleys that led to more desolate structures, each emptier and eerier than the last. An uncomfortable chill hung in the air, gnawing at Steve's nerves until he couldn't hold back any longer.

"Where are we going?" he asked, his voice breaking the silence.

"Oh, you'll see for yourself soon enough." Lucas's tone held an edge that left Steve uneasy.

They took another sharp turn, stopping in front of an isolated building shrouded in shadows, more foreboding than any he'd seen. A shiver ran down his spine; he knew he would never have stumbled upon this place alone.

Then again, when you're trapped here for a thousand years, like Lucas, you have plenty of time to discover every dark corner.

As they reached the door, Steve felt a pang of disappointment—it was locked. But as he inspected the lock, something sparked his memory. It was an unusual shape, one that would fit perfectly with the key he held. He glanced at Lucas, a mix of confusion and suspicion brewing within him.

"How did you know this key would fit this door? And why didn't you mention it sooner?" he asked, his voice barely above a whisper.

Lucas smirked; his expression unreadable. "Patience, Steve. You'll understand everything soon enough. Now, open the door."

The command in Lucas's voice left no room for argument.

Steve did as he was told. The door opened with a creak, disturbing the tense silence surrounding them.

Inside, it was dark. It took him a few moments for his eyes to adjust to the darkness. What he saw then, sent a jolt down his spine.

There was Lexi, tied to a rod, unconscious.

Steve's first instinct was to run towards her. He called her name multiple times. Then, slowly, she opened her eyes.

"Jeff!" her eyes were filled with tears. "How's this possible? I had seen it with my own eyes."

"How....Who did this to you?" he asked, exasperated. "We had solved the mystery; everyone was happy then how did this happen?"

Just then Lucas stepped forward. Lexi looked at him and her eyes filled with hatred and loath. She turned to Steve.

"What are you doing with him?", she asked him sharply.

Steve glanced at Lucas, then back at Lexi, confused. "Lucas? He's... he's my friend. We've been through this together. He's trapped here like us."

Her eyes flared in disbelief. "Friend? Have you lost your mind?" She struggled against her restraints, her voice rising. "He's the one who killed you! He's behind the missing babies!"

Steve shook his head, baffled. "Lexi, you're mistaken. Lucas has been helping me all along. He's one of us!"

At this, Lucas let out a slow, sardonic laugh that echoed around them, cold and sinister, filling the room with a creeping dread. Steve stopped, his heart pounding, and turned to him.

"Lucas," he said, forcing a nervous laugh. "Come on, this isn't funny. Help me untie her."

Lucas's smile faded into a scornful smirk. "Still don't understand, do you?" he said with chilling sarcasm, his voice dripping with menace.

Steve's mind reeled, struggling to grasp the impossible truth unfolding before him. He looked at Lucas, a last sliver of hope clinging to the notion that this was all some cruel joke.

"What... what are you talking about?" he stammered, his voice shaking.

Lucas's lips curved into a dark smile. "You didn't see what happened after the celebration, did you? Let me show you something. Maybe it'll clear things up."

Without warning, a screen materialized in the air before Steve. A scene began to play: it was after the celebrations.

The villagers had dispersed, their laughter and joy now just memories.

Jeff and Lexi were the last to leave, walking under the quiet night sky. Suddenly, the sound of thunderous hooves shattered the silence. A figure on horseback appeared, charging at them like a tempest. The man leapt from his horse, a sword gleaming in his hand, and with a brutal swipe, struck down Jeff.

Steve gasped, transfixed in horror. The dying Jeff lay helpless, his hand stretching out toward Lexi as the stranger seized her. "Liam was just a pawn," the man sneered, dragging her away. "I orchestrated everything." And with that, he rode off, leaving Jeff to his fate—alone, abandoned, the world around him slipping into darkness.

The scene dissolved, and Steve's horrified gaze settled on the face of the attacker: Lucas.

He turned to Lucas, his eyes searching for any sign that this might be some cruel prank. "This...this isn't real. This has to be some mistake."

Lucas smirked, as if Steve's confusion was nothing more than an amusing detail. "Oh, it's real, Steve. Every bit of it."

"Did you really think you'd solved the mystery all on your own? The clues, the memories—they were mine to give," Lucas sneered. "Every twist, every race against time... that was all me, Steve or should I say, Jeff." He stepped closer, his voice dripping with mockery. "The mirror room? The fake Lexi? All mine."

He laughed, low and bitter, watching Steve's face. "You were my perfect little toy."

Lucas leaned closer, savouring every word, his eyes alight with sinister delight. Steve could feel his world unravelling with each revelation, the disbelief twisting his insides as Lucas laid out the web of deception he'd so meticulously spun.

Steve's face hardened, his shock giving way to something darker.

How could I have trusted him? How could I have been so blind?

The realization crashed over him, pulling his disbelief under a tide of rage.

His voice shook with fury. "You... you were the one behind all of it. Every single game. Every single lie," he spat, his words laced with bitterness. "The clues, the memories—you *wanted* me to lose myself, didn't you?"

Lucas's smirk grew wider, as if Steve's anger only validated him.

"At last, you're catching on. I gave you everything you needed to walk right into my trap, and you did—every time."

Steve's fists clenched, and he felt a rage he'd never known build up inside him. "I trusted you. I thought you were my friend; someone I could rely on in this place. But you—you were playing me the entire time."

Lucas shrugged nonchalantly. "Friendship is just another game, Steve. And I play to win."

He gave a slow, mocking smile. "I could have led you right here from the start, you know," he sneered. "But where's the thrill in that? No, I wanted you to remember every step, every detail of this tragic little tale. It wouldn't be fun unless you knew the story... unless you felt every loss."

The words burned in Steve's mind, the betrayal cutting deeper than he could have imagined.

"It was entertaining watching you piece together every clue and every time you tried to save me, you were just inviting trouble for yourself! It was almost laughable. Honestly, I didn't think you had it in you to solve them—but here you are!" he said with a smirk.

Steve squared his shoulders, the disbelief and shock crystallizing into something colder, harder—a resolve to end this, whatever it took.

"Then you're no friend of mine," he said, voice steely. "And I'll make sure you regret ever treating me as your toy.

CHAPTER TWENTY-TWO

A HEART-WRENCHING STORY

"Before you make any move, wouldn't you like to know why I went to all this trouble?" Lucas sneered. "It'd be a shame if you were trapped here forever without even understanding why."

"For money?" Steve shot back, his voice laced with contempt.

"No, my friend, not for money," Lucas said, almost tenderly, as if recounting a bedtime story. "People might think that, but the truth is much darker."

He paused, watching Steve closely. "Remember the vision in the mirror room? The woman burned alive, the baby cast into the river?"

Steve nodded, unease creeping in.

"That baby... was me. And the woman who burned? My mother. A group of men from a nearby village found me just in time, saw the cruelty, and took me to an orphanage. But that place was no better—it was a prison of mockery, pranks, and abuse. I grew up shunned and scarred. When

I finally escaped, I swore I'd uncover the truth about my past."

In spite of the betrayal and anger Steve was experiencing, he couldn't help but feel sorry for Lucas.

Lucas's face darkened as he pointed a finger at Steve and Lexi, accusation burning in his eyes. "I hunted down the men who saved me, and they told me everything. Your people burned my mother because you believed she was cursed, that she'd bring misfortune to your precious village. And from that moment, I swore I'd make you all pay. I wanted the entire village to feel her 'bad luck' a hundred times over."

He straightened, pride flashing across his face, as if unveiling his masterpiece. "I devised a plan, carefully and meticulously, to see every one of you suffer."

"I studied everything about the village," Lucas continued, his voice dripping with pride. "I learned the population, their habits, their weaknesses—every detail that would feed my mission.

It wasn't hard to spot Liam for what he was: a greedy coward willing to do anything for the right price.

So, I had one of my men approach him with a simple proposal— kidnap the village's babies, one by one, for a hefty sum." Lucas gave a self-satisfied nod.

The air inside the building was thick, almost oppressive, as if centuries of secrets pressed against its walls, seeping into the cold stones beneath Steve's feet. Shadows seemed to curl around them, creeping over every inch of the room as Lucas continued his tale. In the silence that hung between Lucas's words, faint creaks and echoes seemed to ripple through the darkness, like whispers of unseen eyes watching.

"My plan was deliberate. Every full moon, a night forever tied to my mother's death, we would take another child. I wanted the village to fear every full moon, to shudder with the same dread they'd caused her. Liam would create the distraction, and my men would slip into the shadows, whisking the babies away through a hidden path in the forest."

Lucas began pacing, his frustration bubbling to the surface. "Everything was going perfectly," he muttered, his tone turning sour.

"Until your brother Michael got curious. Thought he could play the hero, so I made sure he got exactly what he deserved."

He gave a cold laugh, then scowled. "But no—that didn't scare people enough. Then his sister here"—he shot a look of pure contempt at Lexi—"decided to be the next warrior."

He paused, sneering as he recalled Liam's attempts. "To keep the villagers in line, Liam fed them stories about some heroic stakeout, claiming he was on the trail. But even he couldn't keep them away forever," Lucas finished, his disgust evident.

Steve's hands tightened into fists, his mind a whirl of disbelief and denial. How could any of this be real? Every clue, every memory—were they carefully laid traps, nothing more than pawns in Lucas's sick game?

"Then, you know the rest," Lucas continued, his tone laced with satisfaction. "When Liam was arrested and the entire operation fell apart, I couldn't bear the failure any longer. So, I killed Jeffery and captured Lexi. There's a certain poetry in trapping her in the very prison that she had created for me." He laughed triumphantly, savouring the irony.

"But then, you showed up." Lucas fixed his gaze on Steve. "At first, I couldn't believe it—a dead man walking. Curious, I played the friend, piecing together what had happened. When you introduced yourself as Steve and didn't seem to know me, I realized this must be your rebirth." He looked pleased with himself, relishing his own cleverness.

"I saw it as fate giving me a second chance to finish what I started," he said, his voice dropping to a dramatic whisper. "I made sure you remembered every last detail and prepared this little surprise, which I trust you've found... unforgettable."

As Steve listened to this heart-chilling story, a cold realization crept in: if Lucas had orchestrated it all, then every memory Steve held dear, every comforting thought, might be poisoned by his enemy's touch. His chest tightened with betrayal so sharp it hurt. How much of this journey had been his, and how much had been a plaything for Lucas?

And yet... his heart resisted, desperate to cling to the idea of friendship they'd shared, of those moments that had felt genuine. Had it all been a lie? Rage surged as he tried to reconcile the memories with the truth now unfurling before him.

The dim light played tricks, making every flicker a looming figure, every draft a ghostly hand reaching out. A chill crept up Steve's spine as Lucas gave a satisfied laugh, the sound echoing hollowly against the stone, filling the silence with something both sinister and triumphant. In that moment, Steve felt as though he stood at the edge of a dark chasm, unable to see the bottom but knowing it waited to consume him.

CHAPTER TWENTY-THREE

TRAPPED!

"So, I think now it's time to say goodbye," Lucas said, his tone laced with mocking humour.

Steve clenched his fists, attempting to lunge at him, but Lucas raised a finger, halting him with a smirk.

"I don't even need to lift a finger to keep you here, Steve."

"What do you mean by that?" Steve spat, his frustration rising.

"Oh, you'll see soon enough." With that, Lucas gestured, and another screen appeared on the wall.

Steve's eyes widened as he recognized the figures on the screen—his parents. He and his brother, Charlie, were there too, in a park, happily playing while their parents sat nearby, watching them. In the footage, the ball they were tossing flew outside the park. Steve saw his younger self run after it.

But then, a truck barrelled toward him from the side, out of control. His parents' faces twisted in fear as they leapt from the bench, rushing toward him.

Just as they reached him, they shoved him to safety, only to be struck themselves. His younger self had run to his mother, uncertain of what to do. Her final words echoed in his ears as she made him promise to take care of Charlie.

Steve had been saved—but his parents were gone.

Watching this unfold, Steve's expression drained of all colour. "They died...to save me?" he whispered; his voice barely audible. "All this time, I thought it was just an accident."

The scene replayed over and over, an endless loop of his parents' final moments. Steve stood frozen, his mind struggling to process the revelation. His breath became shallow, and his hands trembled, but he didn't move an inch, as if glued to the ground.

Lucas shot a smirk at Lexi, satisfaction glinting in his eyes. "Your hero won't come out of this shock. Goodbye." With that, he turned and vanished into the dark, leaving only the faint sound of a lock clicking shut.

Lexi watched him go, helplessness flooding her as Steve remained paralyzed, trapped in the painful realization of his past.

She called Steve's name again and again, her voice trembling with desperation, but he wouldn't respond. His shoulders were drooped, his body swaying as if he could collapse at any moment. Lexi's mind raced; she had to do something—fast. If this was Jeff's next life and his parents had died saving him, maybe the only thing powerful enough to reach him was a memory from his past life. She closed her eyes, thinking, and then it came to her: the song his mother used to sing, the one he loved so much that even after she passed away, he would hum it to himself whenever he felt sad or missed her.

Swallowing her fear, Lexi began to sing, her voice soft but urgent, every note a plea. At first, Steve didn't react, his eyes still glazed, but as the melody washed over him, he blinked, his gaze shifting slightly. Lexi's heart pounded; she kept singing, her voice steadying, pouring as much warmth and gentleness into each word as she could. His lips parted, as if remembering something distant and comforting, and slowly, he turned his head toward her.

Their eyes met, filled with unshed tears, as if finally finding an anchor.

Lexi continued to sing, her voice a soft, soothing lullaby, as he took a trembling step toward her. Then another. When he reached her, he let out a shuddering breath, his face crumpling as he fell into her arms, gripping her tightly. Lexi leaned her head against his, her own tears falling, and whispered gently that he was safe now. And though she was bound, in that moment, she felt she was holding him closer than ever, sharing his pain, offering him the comfort he needed.

They stayed that way for a while, in a shared silence that felt both comforting and fragile. Eventually, Steve lifted his head, wiping away his tears, and leaned forward to press a gentle kiss to her cheek. "Thank you," he whispered, his voice rough with emotion. Though his words were simple, his eyes held a depth of gratitude that words couldn't capture. He felt himself coming back to reality, grounded by her presence.

"So... how did you end up trapped here? Lucas mentioned this prison was created for him."

Lexi sighed, casting her gaze downward.

"I did create it—to imprison him once and for all. But it was the first time I used such powerful magic. The spell radiated energy beyond my control, and in the moment, I cast it, Lucas held onto me. The magic pulled us both in, and something about this place... it reversed the spell. My powers transferred to him, and while he can't escape, he was able to bind me here indefinitely."

Steve's brow furrowed. "And the train? The one that brought me here?"

"It's a gateway, of sorts. It brings people into this prison world but vanishes after they arrive. It's part of the magic that keeps anyone from easily escaping."

Steve's face brightened slightly. "But since you created this place, you must know a way out, right?"

"It's risky, but not impossible," she said with firm resolve.

"You've been trapped here all this time—didn't you ever try to escape?"

"I watched you die, Jeff. After that, I had no reason to try." She paused, a shadow passing over her face.

"But now we're together." He managed a hopeful smile. "So, how do we escape?"

"We need to capture Lucas," she replied, her voice steady.

CHAPTER TWENTY-FOUR

THE FINAL MOVE

The first part of their plan was freeing Lexi from the iron chains. Steve scanned the room, desperate for anything that could help break her bonds. The chains were clearly enchanted, locked by magic. Suddenly, Lexi's eyes lit up with an idea.

She turned to Steve, saying, "I still have some magic left in me. If I can transfer the magic holding these chains into something else, I might be able to break free. But there's one problem."

"What's that?" Steve asked.

"I can only transfer it to something that belongs to me since I'm the one who cast this magic...and I don't have anything with me."

Steve's mind raced, and then he remembered. When Lucas had asked him to take the key, he had spotted Lexi's locket lying beside it—and taken it along. Now, he was beyond relieved he had. He reached into his pocket, revealing the small locket.

"Will this work?" he asked, holding it up.

Lexi's eyes widened. "Where did you find that? I thought I'd lost it!"

"Well, I found it in one of the memories."

"Memories?" she echoed, intrigued.

"It's a long story," he replied with a small smile. "I'll explain someday."

Steve held the locket to the chains, and Lexi closed her eyes, summoning every bit of magic left in her. For a moment, it seemed nothing was happening, but then the chains began to tremble and gradually loosened.

In a final, quiet clink, they dropped to the floor, and Lexi was free. They shared a brief, fierce embrace, drawing strength from each other before moving forward with the plan.

They exchanged a look of fierce resolve. The hardest part lay ahead: capturing Lucas.

As planned, Lexi began weaving illusions in Lucas's mind, making him see visions of her and Steve attempting a daring escape.

Thanks to the transfer of magic, Lexi had inadvertently established a mental link with Lucas, a connection he was unaware of but one that she had stumbled upon by chance.

Using it, she projected just enough to make the "escape" appear real, feeding his anger and clouding his instincts. Lexi had created an illusion of a concealed escape door at the rear of the building, making it look like they were planning to slip away.

Now, all they had to do was wait and hope that Lucas would fall for the bait, leading him straight into their trap.

The plan was for Lucas to rush into the building to check on them. When Lucas opened the door, Lexi and Steve would be waiting, poised on either side. Lexi would use the last of her magic, and Steve his strength, to capture Lucas with the iron chains. To make the chains hold him, Lexi would have to perform a reverse spell, quickly transferring the magic into them before Lucas sensed the ambush.

Minutes passed by as they took their places, waiting for Lucas to show up.

For some time, they couldn't hear anything except their own heartbeat and breathing but suddenly they heard footsteps. Steve and Lexi's bodies tensed, ready to strike but their tension turned into disappointment when they saw that the one who entered was not Lucas but the soul who was overseeing the memory exchange throughout Steve's journey.

Far away, in his favourite building, Lucas watched as his souls gathered before him, ready to deliver the news of Steve and Lexi' s failed escape attempt.

He found it odd that all of them had come together, but then decided it must be for celebration—an occasion worthy of an audience. He puffed his chest with pride, a smile stretching from ear to ear.

He had known Lexi and Steve were setting a trap, hoping he'd come in person so they could attempt an ambush. They thought they could outsmart him; he mused with a smug smirk. Turning his attention back to the souls, he was surprised to see them inching closer instead of standing at their usual respectful distance.

"It's celebration time, but don't forget I'm still your master. Keep your distance," he commanded firmly.

The souls, however, continued their approach, ignoring his words. Before he could react, they surrounded him, their hands reaching out, gripping him tightly. Confusion flickered across Lucas's face as he felt an unexpected weakness creeping over him.

"What... is this some new form of celebration?" he stammered, baffled, as the souls held him firmly, their eyes vacant yet their grip unyielding. His strength faded, and panic set in as he realized something was terribly wrong.

"What... what are you doing? Get away from me," Lucas commanded weakly, a desperate attempt to regain control. But the strength in his voice was fading, and panic set in as he felt his power slipping.

Just when he thought he would collapse from the encroaching weakness, he looked up to see Steve and Lexi entering the room. His eyes widened in shock.

"You... how can you be here? You're supposed to be..." Lucas stammered, unable to finish his sentence.

"We were supposed to be what—trapped?" Steve replied, his voice edged with contempt.

Lexi stepped forward; her gaze unwavering. "Take him to the room where he imprisoned us. Bind him with the very chains he used to trap me," she commanded. To Lucas's utter disbelief, all the souls turned toward her, bowing in obedience before they began dragging him from the room.

"Wait! No, you're supposed to obey me!" he pleaded, his voice growing frantic. But the souls ignored his cries, their grip firm as they pulled him along.

Once they had him securely bound in the chains, the souls began transferring the remnants of Lucas's magic back to Lexi. With the last of his strength gone, Lucas slumped against the chains, watching helplessly as the souls bowed to Lexi one final time before fading from sight, leaving the building in obedient silence.

Once all the souls had vanished, Steve turned to Lucas, his expression taunting.

"You love showing people stories, don't you? Let's take a look at one about your grand failure."

With a small gesture, Lexi conjured a shimmering screen before Lucas, displaying a scene from earlier in the very room where they stood now. Lucas watched, bound and powerless, as an image of Lexi and Steve began speaking.

"So, how will we capture Lucas?" Steve asked in the scene.

Lexi's voice in the memory was calm but resolute. "It's actually quite simple. We'll make him think he's thwarting our escape. He's too proud to come himself—he'll send the souls. But what he doesn't know is that the souls have a new master: me. Now that I'm free, their loyalty has reverted to their original creator. We'll capture him with his own forces."

The memory faded, leaving the screen blank, and Lexi looked back at Lucas with a triumphant glint in her eyes. "I hope you enjoyed our little surprise, Lucas," she said with a mocking smile.

To their astonishment, Lucas let out a dry, low laugh. "You think this is over? This is just the interval. The game's still on!" And with that, he collapsed into unconsciousness.

Steve and Lexi exchanged glances, dismissing his words as a desperate bluff, a last attempt to mask his defeat. They locked the room securely behind them, leaving Lucas to the darkness.

When they were finally alone, the weight of their journey lifted. They shared a deep, passionate kiss, savouring the freedom they had fought so hard for. With renewed hope, they turned toward the path home, ready to reclaim their lives.

Epilogue

"I have one last piece of the puzzle to solve before we leave," said Steve.

"And what's that?" Lexi asked.

"I was sent here by a group of men to find a girl, but you're the only girl I've seen here."

"You mean, you came here looking for me?"

"It seems so. The question is—why? What do those men want with you?"

Lexi frowned, her mind racing. "It puzzles me too. I think there's only one way to find out!"

As they prepared to go, Lexi couldn't shake the memory of Lucas's last words. *The game is still on.* What did he mean? Did he have an ally working in the shadows, or was he already planning his escape?

Steve's voice cut through her thoughts.

"There's something else bothering me. The mark we kept following—the skull with two crossed bones. I saw it on John's hand, too. The man who first approached me with this job. He must be connected to Lucas somehow."

"You think he's Lucas's ally?" Lexi asked, a sense of unease creeping in.

Steve nodded, feeling his pulse quicken. "It's possible. We need to get to the bottom of this. The answers could be more dangerous than we realize."

With the weight of the unknown pressing on them, Steve and Lexi exchanged a determined look. They stood at the edge of a new journey—one filled with mysteries waiting to be unravelled. Together, they would face whatever lay ahead, ready to confront a game that looked as if it had only just begun.

www.ingramcontent.com/pod-product-compliance
Lightning Source LLC
Chambersburg PA
CBHW051237130726
47988CB00001B/385